Mushroom growing for everyone

Mushroom growing for everyone

ROY GENDERS

FABER AND FABER
London   Boston

First published in 1969
by Faber and Faber Limited
3 Queen Square London WC1
Reprinted 1971, 1974
This revised edition first published
in Faber Paperbacks 1982
Printed in Great Britain by
Fakenham Press Ltd, Fakenham, Norfolk
All rights reserved

© 1969, 1982 Roy Genders

British Library Cataloguing in Publication Data

Genders, Roy
  Mushroom growing for everyone.
  1. Mushroom culture
  I. Title
  635'.8   SB353

  ISBN 0–571–11806–2 Pbk

To John Gledhill

Contents

9

10

Contents

11

Illustrations

Drawings

Drawings by W. A. Genders

Preface to the 2nd edition

Since first beginning mushroom growing in 1931 so much has taken place in commercial mushroom culture that those who were in at the start, so to speak, could never have envisaged the tremendous advancement in growing methods which in fifty years has led to the formation of one of the most profitable industries of Europe and America and one which now provides additional food for those living on the African continent. Whereas fifty years ago a well-produced crop could be expected to yield about 1 lb. of mushrooms for every square foot of compost, today, by following modern cultural methods and using high productive spawns, it is possible to pick 4 or even 5 lb. of mushrooms from every square foot of compost; and even 6 lb. has recently been obtained on a commercial scale. With the retail price of mushrooms rarely falling below £1 a pound, some idea of the big profits to be made is obvious. It is all very different from the early 1930s when commercial culture was in its infancy in Britain, there being little information available as to the proper preparation of the compost and few recognised remedies for many of the pests and diseases which all too often devastated what might have been a profitable crop.

Modern mushroom culture began early in the 1930s when pure culture spawn was first manufactured in Britain. This was in 1932 and shortly before this I had grown my first crop

13

of mushrooms from blocks of field spawn. Those cakes of spawn were of unknown vigour, were often contaminated by pest and disease, and if purchased from garden shops were often several years old. They usually produced only a few brown mushrooms of inferior quality which sold for a shilling a pound and that was all they were worth. The introduction of pure culture spawn, first manufactured in Britain at Shoreham by Messrs. W. Darlington & Sons, was to change all this. One could now rely on the spawn producing a profitable crop of snow-white mushrooms which sold on sight at 2/- (10p) a lb. if growing conditions were right. Then in 1937 the introduction of commercial gypsum in the preparation of the compost which removed the undesirable greasy or 'green' texture gave mushroom growing a further boost. Shortly after came the use of formalin as a disinfectant for washing down mushroom houses and this was another turning point towards achieving heavier crops. Until then, mushroom houses tended to bear smaller and smaller crops, however well the compost was prepared and even when using pure culture spawn. Washing down with formalin after every crop and closing up the house for several days to retain the formaldehyde gas completely eliminated mushroom house 'sickness', and so by 1939, in less than a decade, mushroom culture had become a reliable occupation. Those who had begun growing mushrooms as a hobby took it up on a commercial scale and some made considerable fortunes from the venture. Today, more vigorous, virus-resistant spawns and more reliable insecticides have made mushroom growing even more reliable and still more profitable.

It should be said that there are other proprietary names not mentioned in this book which are equally suitable. Those described are the ones of which I have had personal knowledge during fifty years as a grower.

Preface

My thanks are due to Messrs. W. Darlington & Sons Ltd., now of Rustington, Sussex, who, since they first made pure culture spawn and I came to use it, have guided me through the arts and mysteries of mushroom growing from the early days and have kept me informed of modern cultural methods. To Mr. T. E. Rucklidge of earlier days and to Mr. Benfell and Mr. N. H. Barnard, Technical Director at this time, I am especially grateful for their kindness and help.

In the immediate post war years a number of enthusiastic people from the Irish Republic came for courses of instruction at my mushroom farm and with gratifying results, though much has happened in mushroon growing since then. Over the past decade, the value of the mushroom crop in Eire has increased ten-fold, from £700,000 in 1970 to £7 million in 1980. Much of the credit for this is due to the Irish Mushroom Growers' Association whose members now contribute much to the home economy.

Roy Genders
March, 1981

Introduction

The early growers—food value of the mushroom—physical composition of the mushroom—new spawns

It was Alexander Pope who, in a letter to a friend said of his old home: '. . . the roof is so decayed that after a favourable shower of rain we may, with God's blessing, expect a crop of mushrooms between the chinks of the floors.' There are, however, more certain ways of enjoying a crop of mushrooms at home in this most interesting and profitable of all hobbies.

Much has happened to the mushroom since William Robinson's book on its cultivation, which first appeared a century ago. Robinson's book was called *Mushroom Culture; its Extension and Improvement*, and was the result of a visit he had paid to the Paris growers early in 1868, who were already producing mushrooms on a commercial scale. Robinson mentions that one grower, Monsieur Renaudot, at Mery-sur-oise, nr. Auvers, was then producing 3,000 lb. daily from 20 miles of ridge beds in the local caves, but in Britain, growing was still on a small scale. In the preface to his book Robinson has written: 'I do not hesitate to say that the introduction of the mushroom into our domestic economy in as great a degree as we have it in our power to produce, it would be the addition of a new agent in our cuisine, second to none for its delicacy and unsurpassed for its utility.'

How right was Robinson. Today, mushrooms are one of

17

the most important of all horticultural crops, production in Britain alone being more than 55,000,000 lb. annually, that is, 1 lb. per head of the population, as in the United States of America. Until Britain joined the EEC, production at home was increasing by about $12\frac{1}{2}$ per cent each year, but with the duty on imported mushrooms removed, home production has since remained static. Demand for local grown mushrooms, however, continues to be buoyant, and for those who would like to earn extra money upon retirement, or who would like to increase the weekly wage, or merely to enjoy fresh mushrooms whenever required, mushroom growing at home can be a most satisfying hobby. The mushroom is no longer a food to enjoy only in the autumn, and gone are the days when the cook-housekeeper would not consider using mushrooms before St. Leger day. Today, mushrooms are an all-the-year-round crop and are used by hotels and restaurants in enormous quantities to serve with all kinds of dishes.

Sales from home and farm still provide an outlet for a large percentage of mushrooms produced in Britain and supermarkets now sell millions of pounds annually and are a valuable outlet for growers. As mushrooms are so perishable a crop, there will always be a keen demand for those grown locally, marketed in $\frac{1}{4}$-lb. and $\frac{1}{2}$-lb. punnets and today top quality buttons and cups sell for £1 per pound retail except during the peak summer months. With ever higher wages creating higher standards of living, there are few homes which cannot now afford a few mushrooms each week, and which would prefer to have them in as fresh a condition as possible from a local grower.

Today, provided the grower will follow the simple rules of growing and maintaining cleanliness, mushroom cultivation presents few difficulties, but this was not always so. It was not until 1893 that sterilised, or pure culture, spawn was discovered by the French, its method of production originating at the Pasteur Institute in Paris. It was to revolutionise mushroom growing throughout the world. Hitherto, flake spawn was used. This was dug up from fields in which wild mushrooms were growing, to be replanted in specially made beds of composted manure. In England, this was carried a stage further by inoculating 'bricks', 9 in. × 6 in. × 2 in., made of compressed manure, loam and litter, but by either method the spawn was unreliable, with the mushrooms growing weakly and perhaps not at all, whilst all sorts of pests and diseases were introduced into the beds.

In those days, spawn makers would watch for good flushes of field mushrooms as the modern prospector awaits news of uranium deposits and, as soon as the news reaches him, acts without delay. Finding rich, productive strains was the most important part of spawn making by the brick process. When a good strain was found in the fields, the mycelium was dug up and rushed by train or lorry to the maker, to be planted in a nursery bed which, when permeated by the mycelium, was used to inoculate the bricks. These were moulded out of a mixture of cow and horse manure and sterilised loam. They were then partially dried and inoculated in four or five places with virgin spawn.

At first, the French kept the manufacture of pure culture spawn a closely guarded secret, and it was not until 1900 that the United States Department of Agriculture evolved a method, and not until still later, in 1932, that sterilised spawn came to be manufactured in Britain on a commercial scale. Shortly afterwards came the first tariff on imported mushrooms, and the way was then clear for mushroom growing to begin on a large scale, for the uncertainties had been removed. It was possible to rely on the spawn producing a crop (other things being equal), whilst the grower was assured of obtaining a fair price for his product. But to obtain a crop of mushrooms is very different from obtaining a profitable crop, and to make the venture worthwhile, one should expect at least 2 lb. from each sq. ft. of bed space for which one would expect to receive about £1·50 selling direct to the public. The experienced grower will obtain up to 4 lb. a sq. ft., and in this way mushroom growing can be a highly profitable undertaking, with a quick return on one's outlay.

In Britain, apart from the valuable work of the Mushroom Growers' Association, there has been little official encouragement for growers, unlike America, where several universities have set up special departments for scientific mushroom cultivation. In the state of Pennsylvania alone, production is estimated at 100,000,000 lb. annually, and it continues to increase throughout the United States and Canada at about 10 per cent annually.

Food value of the mushroom

The mushroom has a higher mineral salt content than beef or mutton, and almost twice that of any other vegetable, whilst its protein value is double that of asparagus, cabbage and potatoes, four times that of tomatoes and carrots, and six times that of oranges. It contains the salts of iron, copper, potassium and calcium, whilst it is also rich in vitamin B, and in vitamin D, the sunshine substitute. The mushroom also has a good supply of enzymes, particularly trypsin, which is a valuable aid to digestion, and is the same enzyme as that derived from pancreatic juices.

It is of interest to compare the composition of various foods in relation to the mushroom, as in the table on the following page.

In addition to the food value of the mushroom, there is nothing to waste, the base of the stem having been trimmed before marketing. A further advantage is that, being devoid of starch, the mushroom is an ideal food for diabetics, and for anyone not wishing to put on weight. Far from being a delicacy, boiled in milk, mushrooms are a nourishing meal, especially for invalids, for they are easily digested.

FOOD	WASTE	PROTEIN	CARBO-HYDRATES	FUEL VALUE
Mushroom	0	3·5	6·8	210
Apple	25	0·3	10·8	220
Banana	35	0·8	14·3	300
Beef	10	19·2	—	670
Cabbage	15	1·4	4·8	125
Carrot	20	1·0	7·4	160
Chicken	40	12·6	—	300
Fish	50	9·2	—	380
Grape	25	1·0	14·4	335
Onion	10	1·4	8·9	205
Orange	27	0·6	8·5	170
Pork	25	15·0	—	900
Potato	5	1·8	14·7	302
Tomato	2	1·0	4·0	105

A discovery of importance was made before World War II by Dr. Williams, of Texas University, when he found that the great human body requirement, folic acid, was present in mushrooms as well as in yeast, liver and spinach, but in a far larger quantity in the mushroom. This acid is given when treating all forms of anaemia, and at once the mushroom was in great demand in America for treating this condition. No longer was the mushroom looked upon as a luxury food.

The American nutritionist Dr. Benjamin Frank believes that premature ageing is due to a deficiency in the body of RNA. To maintain required amounts, he suggests a high intake of sardines, shellfish or mushrooms.

In Britain alone, there exist more than 5,000 different

species of fungi, of which at least a thousand are edible. No more than a dozen are really poisonous—*Amonita phalloides*, the death cap, is the most dangerous of all. The horse mushroom (*Psalliota arvensis*), sold chiefly from costermongers' carts, is sometimes used as a substitute for the field mushroom (*Psalliota campestris*), and in France truffles are almost as popular as field mushrooms, but with production of the cultivated mushroom now on so large a scale, there is little interest taken in other forms. It may be said here, that there are those to whom the mushroom acts as a mild poison, as do some other fungi, and where this is so the mushroom should not be consumed. A small quantity of olive oil taken immediately after eating will usually prevent deterioration of one's condition, or for that matter, whenever any fungus is consumed which does not agree with one's system.

Physical composition of the mushroom

The life cycle of the mushroom may be divided into three stages: (i) the spores or seeds; (ii) the mycelium or spawn growth, and (iii) the fruit—the mushroom itself. Unable to make carbohydrates from the carbon dioxide of the air, fungi are dependent upon other plants (or animals) for their survival. The mushroom breathes by taking in oxygen and exhaling carbon dioxide, thus following exactly the opposite process from ordinary plant life, though it reproduces itself in exactly the same way as plants from seed.

The mushroom growing in a field passes from the early button stage to that of the fully opened fruit in four to five days, gradually bursting through the annulus, or veil, which is formed between the cap and stalk on the underside, until the cap eventually becomes flat with the gills exposed. These gills produce spores in the same way as a plant produces seeds, and if an open mushroom is placed, gills down, on a

sheet of white paper and allowed to remain in position for
48 hours, the exact form of the gills will be reproduced by
minute spores which have fallen from them. In the field, these
spores fall amongst grass and decayed leaves, and are eaten
by horses, to pass out in the droppings and appear again
eventually as the fruiting body, the mushroom.

A mushroom is composed of these parts:

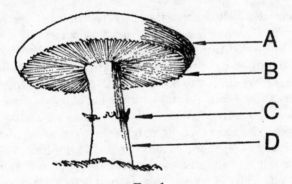

FIG. 1
(A) The cap, or pileus (B) the gills, or lamelae (C)
the veil, or annulus (D) the stalk, or stipe.

There has always been a certain prejudice by some people
against mushrooms produced artificially; for their argument
they contend that field-grown mushrooms are greatly superior
to those artificially produced. This is not so as, though the
open brown mushroom of pastureland has a superior flavour
to button mushrooms produced indoors or for that matter in
fields, it has less food value, whilst those mushrooms growing
naturally are usually troubled by attacks from mushroom
flies, which lay their eggs in the gills; these hatch to produce
grubs which feed upon the mushrooms, tunnelling through
cap and stalk. This may be prevented when they are growing

23

indoors by the regular use of non-poisonous sprays. With the horse population diminishing yearly, the number of field mushrooms has also diminished, whilst the procuring of supplies of horse manure for artificial production has also become more and more difficult, so that it has been necessary to find and bring into use other growing media.

New spawns

During the 1970s, new strains of spawn have increased cropping. *Agaricus bisporus*, the one most commonly grown, is a two-spored variety of the cultivated mushroom and has been improved by selection since its introduction early in the 1930s, as it is difficult to breed from only two spores for most spores are self-fertile with two nucleii. The Horst Research Station, however, have raised a four-spored variety, *A. bitorquis*, the spores having only one nucleus so breeding is now easier. This spawn is also immune to mushroom virus, commonly known as La France disease (see page 198). It is, however, difficult to use and is best left to experienced growers as it needs a pasteurised compost and a temperature of 76° F (25° C) in which to grow, and few growers can provide these conditions. A royalty is paid to the Horst Research Station where spawn is produced under licence. On all pure culture spawns a small index-linked levy is paid to the Mushroom Growers' Association who use the money for mushroom publicity.

1—Where mushrooms can be grown

Growing at home—outlay and returns—where to grow mushrooms—obtaining the materials

It may be said that mushrooms can be grown by almost anyone, almost anywhere. William Robinson has told of the
Belgian cook who grew a dish of mushrooms in a pair of
wooden shoes, and when on Royal Air Force service, the
author grew mushrooms in boxes beneath his bed and in a
locker; when handed in at the cookhouse they made a tasty
addition to the monotony of the stews. Mushrooms have no
colouring matter and so do not need sunlight to obtain the
requisite nutriment for survival. They will grow in total darkness where no other crop would flourish, hence any of those
unwanted places about the home or outbuildings, which
would perhaps be of no value for any other purpose, may be
made productive. But total darkness is not essential for growing mushrooms. However, though light is not necessary,
since fungi have exactly the opposite functions to green
plants and do not need light to make chlorophyll, sunlight
should be excluded for, if shining directly on to the beds, it
will cause the casing to dry out too quickly and will also cause
cracking of the mushroom caps, which will reduce their
market value.

A crop of mushrooms may be produced in boxes beneath
the kitchen sink, in a cellar or in a garden shed. They may be

grown in a cupboard beneath the stairs, or in an attic room, where perhaps no more than two or three boxes may be planted with spawn; these would take the minimum amount of time to care for, just a few minutes each day. When the crop came into bearing and, provided the temperature did not fall below 45° F (7° C) there would be a few mushrooms each week for possibly three months or more. Artificial heat is not necessary for mushrooms, but the beds (or boxes) will not bear if the temperature falls below 40° F (4° C). Though the beds may become completely frozen, no harm will be done, and the crop will begin again as soon as the air temperature rises. This is another advantage in growing mushrooms in comparison with plants which may be damamged by hard frosts. Indeed, the best quality mushrooms will be obtained where the temperature does not rise above 55° F (13° C), and a cool place is better than one which is too warm, when pest and disease will be at a minimum.

Mushrooms may also be grown in such places as a verandah or terrace, or in a courtyard, with the boxes stacked against a wall to give protection from wind and rain and to ensure that they will be more secure. In these places the boxes may be made up in April, and will begin to crop before the end of May, continuing until late summer, when the indoor boxes will be ready and will carry on the succession. Boxes may be moved without much trouble, and may be made up outdoors to be taken inside for cropping at almost any time. There is no unpleasant smell with correctly composted manure, and no mess. The boxes will require only the minimum of moisture, just sufficient to prevent the spawn from drying out. It is quite wrong to believe that watering will cause trouble indoors, and fears of water seeping through the floor to the room below need not be entertained. Excess moisture will kill the growing spawn and must be avoided at all costs.

Where mushrooms can be grown

Many growers have started with the very smallest area and, finding their hobby interesting, have gradually extended into making their venture almost a full-time occupation. Mushrooms can be grown in or near the home, so that they may be cared for by those who have retired, or by the housewife. Demanding only an hour or so each day, they may be grown by those working full time as a means of increasing their income, and who are prepared to attend to the main operations during weekends.

Growing in the dark, mushroom beds are not subject to rapid changes of temperature as are crops growing under glass, and which demand almost hourly care with their ventilation and with their moisture requirements. However, the grower of 1,000 sq. ft. or more will need to give the venture almost all his time, for picking and marketing the crop will require daily attention, and there will be in addition such routine tasks as clearing the beds of roots and filling in the subsequent holes as well as watering, and applying insecticides and fungicides.

Where growing on a small scale at home, sales may be made to neighbours and to local shops without travelling very far and without the need for transport, but as one extends, there will be the need to travel further afield; then one must remember that, as mushrooms quickly deteriorate, they need to be marketed with the minimum of delay. If there could be a member of one's household in attendance during the day, callers could be encouraged, which would reduce delivery time to a minimum.

Outlay and returns

What of returns? Those growing only a small area would be satisfied to obtain sufficient returns from local sales to pay for the mushrooms consumed by their household, and for the cost of materials. Where growing on a larger scale, one will expect to be financially rewarded for one's outlay and time. An area of 500 sq. ft. yielding 2 lb. a sq. ft. will, at 20p per quarter pound return £800. Two crops a year would double that sum and could earn the grower about £30 a week less expenses.

The outlay would depend upon a number of factors. If growing in trays, in the form of fish boxes, obtainable direct from the manufacturers at Fleetwood, Hull or Grimsby, these will be of a size to cover an area of about 5–6 sq. ft. They may be handled unfilled by a person working alone, and when filled with compost, may easily be moved by two people. As about 48 boxes would be required for a worthwhile crop, these would cost £20 or so, but have the advantage that they would remain in use for several years, for at least eight crops. The cost per crop would be only £2·50, or 10p a sq. ft., which is capable of yielding £3 worth of mushrooms.

The compost, whether of horse manure or of poultry manure, or made from an artificial activator, would cost about £10 for 48 boxes, and £2 could be allowed for additional straw. Six bags of manure spawn at £1 each, and approximately £2 for fungicides needed for sterilising the boxes between crops and for a small amount of gypsum to mix with the compost, will give a total outlay in the region of £20 per crop. Thus, an average crop will show a most useful profit.

There will be certain 'tools of the trade' to purchase, including a fork for turning the compost, and a hot-bed thermometer (if growing on a scale to warrant its purchase). The commercial grower will need a soil- and manure-testing outfit, which is quite inexpensive to buy, and easy to use. A pair of rubber gloves for inserting the spawn will protect the hands. But, apart from a fork, none of these requirements is essential unless growing on a commercial scale, though one should have access to a supply of clean water which will be needed in the preparation of the compost and for watering the beds.

Where to grow mushrooms

To make use of existing space, trays may be stacked around a cellar or garage. If these are built of stone or brick, the air temperature will be cool in summer and warm in winter. It may only be possible (owing to size of car) to have the trays stacked down one side of a garage, but stacked in eight rows of six almost to the roof, it would still be possible to accommodate 48 trays.

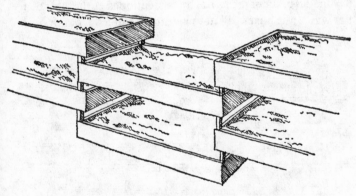

FIG. 2

Method of stacking trays in a garage or shed; in this way space is utilised to the best advantage and at the same time adequate air circulation is permitted.

One could also stack the same number of trays against the outside of the wall for a summer crop, and by leaving the car out during the summer months, the cropping area in the garage could be greatly increased. As many dwellings are now installed with oil or gas fired central heating, it is usual to extend this at little extra cost to the garage, and this would ensure a winter crop even if the outside temperature fell to zero.

Those who would wish to make use of the walls of a court-yard for a summer crop could either stack the trays against the wall, preferably on the sunless side, or else 'window boxes' could be constructed with ¾-in. timber and fastened (with brackets) at intervals to the wall. It will be necessary to leave 6 in. between the top of one and the base of another to allow for filling with the compost and picking the crop. The boxes should be made 2½ ft. long and 9 in. wide, and they should be 8–9 in. deep, the same as the trays mentioned earlier. Made to this width, the boxes will not protrude too much from the wall.

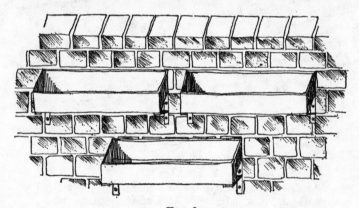

FIG. 3
'Window boxes' or trays fastened to the wall with brackets.

When making the boxes, or constructing one's own trays, it is preferable to use western red cedarwood, which is both

30

strong and durable. The local timber merchant will cut the wood to the desired length; the ends should fit inside and this must be allowed for when estimating the length. If any attempt is made to dovetail the corners, it should be remembered that the strength of a dovetail lies in the perfection of its construction, and a water-resistant glue should be used. When securing the two ends, no advantage will be gained by using screws instead of 2-in. nails, but for additional strength at the corners, an angle bracket should be screwed either inside or outside the box. Adequate air holes of $\frac{1}{2}$ in. diameter should be made in the base.

After the boxes have been made, they should be treated with an organic solvent-type preservative, preferably based on copper naphthanate, and then allowed to stand out in the open for a week or so, to become 'weathered' before being filled with compost. Tar oil washes should not be used as wood preservatives where mushrooms are being grown.

Another method of obtaining a crop is to erect, at the base of a wall, a wooden frame 3 ft. wide and of any length. Old railway sleepers may be used for the sides or 12-in. boards, held in place by pegs driven into the ground. As light is not necessary, frame lights can be made of wooden laths covered with black thermo-plastic sheeting to keep out the rain and the direct rays of the sun, or, if laths are fixed across the frame, a tarpaulin sheet can be placed over them to keep the sheet above the growing mushrooms. It is a simple matter to roll back the sheet when the beds are to be attended to, and to replace it after the mushrooms have been gathered and the beds watered.

Those making use of a cellar or outhouse, as is often the case on older property, could save expense by making up the beds directly on the ground, but this has its disadvantages, and also not nearly so large an area can be utilised as when

31

trays (or boxes) are used. Here, the compost can be prepared under cover if required, and the work done in the evening where lighting is available.

Where women or older people are to take up mushroom cultivation, it should be the aim from the beginning to have everything so arranged that the work will be manageable. One is often asked, is the work too hard? Thoughts of preparing large quantities of compost and filling innumerable boxes seem rather daunting at first, but there need be no fear of the work proving too strenuous. Strawy compost is quite light to prepare and to place in boxes. It is then made firm and is ready for spawning. At the appropriate time, it is given a thin covering of peat and chalk, or of peat and sterilised loam, and this finishes the work necessary, apart from giving an occasional watering, and gathering the crop. It is an ideal crop for the husband-and-wife team who may, at some time, wish to take up mushroom growing to augment the weekly income.

If no suitable place can be found for growing mushrooms, a small shed erected at the bottom of the garden or at the side of the house will be ideal for growing a crop in trays, and there will be no fear of damaging the shed. Several of our largest growers began in this way, adding more shed space each year and using electricity taken from the house for heating and lighting during winter, when mushrooms are in most demand and prices usually higher than in summer. From this, the next step is a specially designed mushroom house, which it may be possible to erect on one's own land or, in the case of those living in the country, on land rented from a local farmer or smallholder.

Country dwellers will be at an advantage in finding suitable buildings to grow mushrooms. A disused poultry house, repaired and made clean, will be suitable, and on most farms

Where mushrooms can be grown

there will be a barn or shed capable of growing a crop with the minimum of attention. For this reason, the farmer or smallholder could utilise many an unused building and from it make a handsome profit. There is also labour available for large scale preparation of the compost, whilst manure from horse or poultry, and clean straw, is to be had at the minimum of cost.

The poultry farmer, especially, is suitably placed for mushroom growing, for heavy crops are to be obtained from poultry manure which is usually put to no profitable use. Indeed, the production of eggs and of mushrooms would be complimentary to each other, for with both there are similar outlets with sales to supermarkets, farm shops and butchers. Also, the same housing with its artificial lighting, can be used both for poultry and for mushrooms, alternating one with another so that disease is kept to a minimum. One thousand hens and 1,000 sq. ft. of mushrooms can be accommodated within a very small area.

Where horses are kept, for instance at such establishments as riding schools, then mushroom growing presents few difficulties, for a supply of manure will be always available. A crop may be grown in outbuildings or unused stables, using trays or by erecting shelves around the walls. This method may also be carried out in a cellar or shed or an outside washhouse, most of which have become redundant with the installation of the indoor washing machine and gas- or oil-fired central heating.

A mushroom crop may alternate with a tomato crop in a greenhouse, and all that is necessary is to darken the glass. The beds may be made up on the floor of the house or trays may be stacked down the centre of the house, allowing space all round to tend the trays. The trays may be made up outside and carried in for stacking, or the compost may be given

33

its final turn under glass and the trays stacked before filling. Some greenhouse mushroom growers make use of flat
beds placed directly on the ground; alternatively others make
up double ridge beds. The latter will increase the area of
cropping whilst taking up less space on the ground, but they
also require more compost to make up.

Trays have the advantage in several ways. A larger cropping area may be obtained and so will make more economical
use of the heating and, as warm air rises, the trays will obtain
greater warmth than ground beds and will begin to crop
earlier. Again, ground beds are more liable to be troubled by
disease unless the top soil is removed before the beds are
made up each time. Also, it is possible, when using trays, to
bring on the crop by placing them in a shed or mushroom
house until the greenhouse has been cleared of the tomato
crop, about the middle to end of September, when the trays
can be moved in and will come into bearing almost at once.
In this way it will be possible to take off two crops during the
winter months.

The compost should be ready for spawning about September 1st, and if gentle heat is maintained, the beds will commence to crop towards the end of October and will continue
in bearing until early March, when the house is emptied and
cleaned, and made ready for the tomato plants. To minimise
loss of heat, the glass may be covered on the inside with
plastic sheeting or with strips of hessian canvas, either of
which are readily removed, together with the shading, when
the crop has finished.

Fibre-glass may also be used to insulate the outside of a
glasshouse roof, and is especially effective if bitumen bonded,
or it may be made weather-proof by covering it with roofing
felt. It will provide valuable insulation as well as darkness,
and will greatly reduce the cost of fuel during winter.

Where mushrooms can be grown

The nurseryman who can use the spent mushroom compost on the land, will find it a valuable source of plant food and humus, in addition to its being easily workable. It is also valuable for pot plants and as a fertiliser for lawns, and its original cost will be covered by its use after cropping.

Fertiliser value of mushroom compost
(Figures are given in percentage of dry material)

	FRESH MANURE	MUSHROOM COMPOST
Ammonium nitrogen	0·4	0·15
Water insoluble protein	7·5	11.25
Total nitrogen	1·5	2·30
Lignin	15·0	16·50
Cellulose	30·0	13·00
Minerals	12·7	38·00

Wherever mushrooms are to be grown in old buildings, the walls and roof should be made as airtight as possible. Stone and brick walls should be rendered with cement on the inside. This will not only prevent draughts from reaching the beds, but will ensure that fumigation against pests is effective; this would not be so where the gas released by fumigating compounds is allowed to escape. Treatment of old walls will also prevent pests from seeking refuge during fumigation and during the life of the crop.

Often with old sheds, the roof timbers are exposed and here, too, will be a breeding ground for pest and disease. In addition, valuable heat will be lost in winter and as warm air rises, it will be those beds nearest the ground which will suffer most. A false roof may be constructed of plaster on hardboard with the minimum of expense.

Open sheds, probably housing implements or tools, can be used for growing mushrooms, making the beds either on the floor or in trays stacked round the three sides. Cold winds can be excluded by covering the trays with polythene sheeting or by draping bitumen-treated hessian down the open side. This will also maintain darkness. The use of polythene sheeting is most valuable for covering the trays, for it will prevent the rapid loss of heat from the compost and of moisture from the casing soil.

Disused railway carriages, and single-deck buses, which have had their windows filled in, may be used to grow mushrooms, whilst rhubarb sheds are also suitable, either making the beds directly on the ground or stacking the trays in rows. As the rhubarb is usually forced as a winter crop, the mushrooms will occupy the sheds only during summer months and as direct sunlight is excluded for the rhubarb crop, the sheds will require no further attention other than the maintenance of adequate ventilation. This is important wherever mushrooms are grown for Dr. Lambert, head of the Bureau of Plant Industry at Maryland, in the United States of America, has shown that as little as 5 per cent of carbon dioxide in the atmosphere will retard the growth of the mushrooms but not of the mycelium, whilst half that concentration will cause the mushrooms to grow light and long-stemmed. A heavy, stagnant atmosphere is the cause of more failures amongst mushroom growing than any other factor. Mushrooms must have a free circulation of fresh air and preferably a temperature which does not rise above 60° F (16° C), though during the height of summer this is often exceeded. Incidence of attacks from pests and diseases will also be greater when the temperature exceeds 60° F (16° C), whilst the beds will require more attention to their watering. For this reason many growers so arrange the crops that there will be few mushrooms during the months of July and August, except where growing near holiday resorts when demand will be heavy. The mushroom growing site that can provide conditions as near as possible to those expected by the commercial grower will simplify the management and bring greater rewards.

With the re-alignment of the Lancashire textile trade, a large number of mills of all sizes and shapes have become unoccupied during recent years and are unsuitable for using for almost any purpose other than for poultry and mushroom growing, for which they are ideal on a large scale. Many of these mills are situated near to a railway station and usually on a good road with easy access to thickly populated areas where the crops would find a ready sale.

The author was asked to superintend the filling of one small mill which had been taken over by several ladies to be run as a joint enterprise, and very profitable their business has become. Three people are concerned with the venture, one keeping the books and doing all the clerical work; another obtaining orders and delivering the mushrooms to stores and supermarkets; whilst a third takes care of crop production, which can be managed by one person once the beds are made. Floor beds are used, and the compost is prepared and the beds made up by two farm workers who are happy to sacrifice several weekends during the year for a suitable reward. They also remove the compost when the crop has finished. The three ladies are quite able to manage the rest of the work, and with 3,000 sq. ft. and two crops a year, they are left with £4,000 a year after paying for rent and rates, heating, labour and the cost of spawn and compost; also containers and delivery charges. They each take £20 a week, using the balance to increase their area and they work only in the mornings, doing their housework and shopping in the afternoons. The work provides an interest and pays for many things about the home which they could not otherwise afford.

Another method by which mushrooms can be produced

37

and which may be worthy of consideration is the plastic 'house', first used at the National Vegetable Research Station at Wellesbourne in Warwickshire. This was made by sealing a plastic sheet and inflating it, and if this is used, it should be erected preferably over a concrete floor, for cleanliness. Black plastic material may be used and fastened to a timber frame built of sufficiently strong wood to withstand gale force winds; this could provide accommodation for a mushroom crop grown in boxes. The plastic should last for up to ten years and, if treated with preservative, the timber should last almost indefinitely, providing a cheap and trouble free way of growing mushrooms. It is to be recommended where pasteurisation can be carried out in a specially sealed and heated building and the boxes transferred afterwards.

One is often asked by those thinking of taking up mushroom cultivation, and who would like some practical experience before doing so, whether it is possible to attend a course of instruction. A number of commercial growers take pupils, usually for a week at a time spread over a period so that knowledge may be gained concerning all aspects of cultivation. For a course lasting a week much may be learned, whilst there are growers who, when time permits and for a small fee, will travel to the intending grower to give instruction in matters of housing and in the preparation of the compost and making up the beds.

Obtaining the materials
One is often asked, how does one obtain the manure so essential for mushroom growing? This presents no difficulty. The home grower will be able to obtain a few bales of straw from a corn merchant or farmer, some poultry manure and a bag of activator, possibly Adco 'M', a preparation specially made for mushroom growing. It may be used either by itself

and mixed with the straw, when it has the advantage of being free from pests, or it may be used in a smaller quantity with poultry manure; where obtainable, it can be mixed with horse manure, which is now available only from racing or riding stables. A heavily cropping compost can be made from straw and chemicals, though the addition of animal manure will give the compost 'body' and will make for more satisfactory preparation of the compost. Poultry manure (in the dry state) is readily available, and may be obtained by rail if there is not a local source of supply, so that the question of a suitable growing medium need cause no worry. The commercial grower, however, must be assured of adequate supplies before making a start. Supplies are often available from local riding schools, who will keep the manure under cover if you mention that you want it for mushroom growing, as in this case it should be protected from heavy rain. Those who grow mushrooms on a larger scale should contact one of the breweries who still use heavy horses for advertisement purposes at the agricultural shows. Alternatively contact Burcros Composts, Clarks Farm, Darby Green, Camberley, Surrey (telephone: Yateley 872241), who can usually supply large quantities in various stages of composting.

Wherever mushrooms are to be grown, conditions of the utmost cleanliness should be provided. Where extending one's operations from a few boxes in the home to the use of a shed, garage or outhouse, the elimination of all likely sources of trouble should be urgently considered, for the compost, and the conditions of warmth and humidity under which mushrooms are grown, are ideal for the breeding of pests and diseases, and if these are not kept under control will bring destruction to what might otherwise have been a most valuable crop.

2—Growing at home

Materials for home growing—preparing the compost—filling the boxes—spawning—small packs in the home

When starting to grow mushrooms at home in a garage, shed or cellar, as many boxes should be made up as can be conveniently managed at one time. For one thing, it will be more economical and will take up little more time to fill a dozen boxes as it will to fill two or three, whilst it is far more satisfactory to prepare a compost to fill a dozen than only a few boxes. This is because the larger the compost heap, the more heat it will generate; and the greater the bacterial action, the more rapidly will the straw break down.

For this reason also, it is suggested that, where possible a small quantity of dry poultry manure be added to the heap when first made up. It will carry no unpleasant smell and will not only increase bacterial activity but, with its high nitrogen content, will increase the yield of the compost. A 28-lb. bag of poultry manure, obtainable from most poultry breeders, will be sufficient to make a compost to fill a dozen trays, each of 5–6 sq. ft. The poultry manure may be stored in a dry place until ready for use, and likewise the activator, which is needed to break down the straw and provide nutrition for the spawn to feed upon.

Upon the correct preparation of the compost will depend the weight of the crop. A well-prepared compost may yield

2 lb. of mushrooms per sq. ft., whereas one badly prepared may yield no more than $\frac{1}{2}$ lb. But like the experienced cook and her cakes, a good compost is achieved only by intelligent practice.

Adco 'M' is a suitable activator, and there are others. The 'M' is important, for this is not the same Adco as used for rotting down garden rubbish but is specially prepared for mushroom composts. It may be used on its own with straw or, and this is preferable, mixed with poultry or horse manure which will give 'body' to the compost. The best crop of mushrooms the author ever grew was from a load of elephant manure obtained from a travelling circus. It yielded nearly 4 lb. per sq. ft. and a free seat for the show also went with it, so it was altogether a profitable venture.

It is important that the compost attains a temperature of at least 160° F (71° C) in the heap so that the spores of vert-de-gris disease and brown plaster mould are killed. A high temperature will also drive any mushroom midges to the surface, where they may be killed by one of the mushroom fly sprays. It should be said that, where animal manures are excluded, relying entirely upon the activator and possible a little poultry manure for composting, the incidence of introducing disease spores will be minimised.

A high temperature and ample bacterial activity in the heap will also produce a more evenly-textured growing medium of the correct moisture content, which will retain its heat for a time when the trays have been made up. The spawn will then become established more quickly, before adverse factors can take over and it will be able to make full use of the nutritional value of the compost. Adco 'M' and any other activator will also be constant in its food content and will make for a more evenly composted heap. Horse manure, often exposed to heavy rain, will vary considerably in its food

41

content and also in other respects, for much will depend upon what the horses have been fed. Even the type of horse plays its part. Manure from the old brewery draught horses, which is now rarely to be obtained, would produce a heavier mushroom and a larger crop than the manure from the lighter ponies and race horses now obtainable from riding schools and racing stables.

To fill a dozen boxes (60–70 sq. ft.) two 1-cwt. bales of wheat straw should be obtained, and to mix with it, 14 lb. of Adco 'M' in addition to the 28 lb. of poultry manure mentioned previously. If this is not available, it would be advisable to use an additional 7 lb of activator. Do not mix any soil with the compost for fear of introducing disease spores. At one time, it was usual to add a small quantity of soil to soak up the ammonia fumes, but it is now known that these are important in the fermentation process, and the risk of introducing disease with the soil is too great to take.

For the same reason, never prepare the compost on an earth floor. It should be done on a clean cement floor or on the stone floor of a shed or cellar. If it is not possible to prepare the compost under cover, then make use of a corner formed by the two adjoining walls of a yard to turn the compost against. This will prevent strong winds from drying out the compost and will enable it to be more easily protected from heavy rain whilst heating up.

Preparing the compost
When the straw arrives, shake out each bale, at the same time soaking it thoroughly with water. It could be left for a day or two, allowing it to take in rain water, or by giving more water if the weather is dry. It will be surprising just how much moisture fresh straw will take up, and it is better to add almost all that is necessary at this time so as not to

wash out the activator after it has been added. Before making up the heap, obtain from a builder's merchant 7 lb. of powdered pink gypsum (calcium sulphate). This should be added to the straw as the heap is made, to prevent it becoming sticky and greasy. It will also give greater aeration. Gypsum costs only a few pence a pound and should never be omitted.

As soon as one is ready to start, spread out a quantity of straw to a depth of 12 in., making the base of the heap about 5 ft. square. It is desirable to make the heap as high as possible for it will then generate the maximum of heat and will also be less troubled by wind and rain. If the straw is still dry, give more water, and then sprinkle uniformly over the first layer sufficient activator, poultry manure and gypsum for each to fill a garden trowel. There will be no smell, and no trouble in their application.

Then add another 12-in. layer of straw, and repeat the procedure until all the straw and the fertilisers have been used up. By this time the heap will have reached a height of about 6 ft., and should have the top rounded off with straw so that as much rain as possible will run off in showery weather. It will help, in this respect, if the top is covered with old sacks; these will also help it to heat up and retain its heat. Though the compost needs air to assist in bacterial activity, drying winds do no good, and the heap should be protected from them as much as possible.

Within 48 hours, the heap will have begun to generate considerable heat, by which time it will have sunk by about 12 in. The heating shows that the heap has been correctly made and that bacterial activity has commenced. If all is well, by the fourth day the temperature will reach 160° F (71° C), and any disease spores present will be destroyed. The temperature will then begin to fall and the heap should be turned. This will usually be after about six days.

The compost should be shaken out to a base of similar dimensions, and if any parts appear dry, water should be sprinkled on them, but not in so large a quantity as to wash away the activator. This first turn is most important in the production of the compost, for the various preparations will now be mixed into the whole amount of straw, and the greater the care taken, the better will be the compost.

It may be said here that chaff can be used instead of straw, but I have never found this to heat up as well in the heap. Again, there will be no unpleasant smell, only a warm mushroomy aroma. So that every part of the heap will attain the same high temperature, it is advisable to turn the outside to the inside, and this will also ensure that all parts are in contact with the activator. The outer portions of the heap will usually be drier, and will take up more moisture when at the centre of the heap. If there are grey patches to be seen in the straw, this is a sign of 'burning', probably due to excessive dryness, but there is no need to worry for, if sprinkled with water, much of it will have disappeared by the time the compost is ready to be put into the boxes. Throughout the operation, shake out the compost thoroughly, disentangling any long straw, and re-build the heap with the sides as upright as possible. Then round off the top and cover with sacks.

Again, the heap will heat up as before and will be ready for a second turn after six more days. By now it will be turning a rich brown colour as the moist straw absorbs the activator, and the aroma of mushrooms will be even stronger. With the next turn, no more water should be given unless there are dry patches, and then only sparingly. Yet another turn will be necessary until the compost has become a deep mahogany brown colour, and when it has again reached peak temperatures, it will be ready to place in the trays or boxes.

44

Growing at home

The compost should never have a black appearance, for this will mean a greasy compost which, when in the beds or trays, will quickly become cold and will set solid like lard, thus cutting off the air needed by the growing spawn. Instead, it should be open in texture and just moist enough to bind together when squeezed in the hand (a rubber glove can be used). No excess moisture should exude between the fingers, yet it should leave behind a coating of moisture on the hand (or glove). Spawn cannot live in a too wet compost, but there must be sufficient moisture present to support its growth and this moisture must be retained throughout the life of the crop. It is not possible to water the compost after spawning, for fear of harming the growing spawn. If, at the final turn, the compost appears too wet and tends to be greasy, another 7 lb. of gypsum should be sprinkled on and mixed into the compost. There need be no fear of using an excess, for spawn seems to grow with extra vigour whenever in contact with gypsum.

For the townsman, poultry manure is readily obtained through postal advertisers; also Adco 'M', and most town houses have a cellar, garage or back yard (or garden) where the compost can be cured. However, where these facilities are not available, it is usually possible to obtain the services of a nurseryman who would prepare the compost to one's requirements and deliver for a small charge.

Filling the boxes

It will take about three weeks to prepare the compost after which it can be made up into beds or used to fill boxes; this should be done without delay for, if it becomes over-composted, the growing medium will begin to show an acid reaction—to a chemical test—and will not only begin to lose heat but also its food value, resulting in a reduced crop. If anything, slightly under-composted manure is better than that which is over-composted. The commercial grower will know exactly when the correct time has come to spawn by making acidity/alkaline tests daily, and these will confirm what the physical quality of the compost may have begun to indicate, namely, that it is right for spawning. It should be said that when ready to use, the long straw should have become broken down so that it is quite short and should readily break apart when twisted in the hands.

If it is required to have an all-the-year supply, then the boxes (or beds) should be made up two or three times a year, but much will depend upon whether some artificial warmth is available for winter cropping. For an outdoor crop or for an unheated shed, the first composting should commence early in March when the worst of the winter weather is over. The beds will be ready for spawning about April 1st and will begin to crop by mid-May, finishing in August. Preparation of more compost should take place during that month so that the beds are ready to spawn before the month-end. The spawn will have run through the compost by mid-September and by the month-end, with the weather continuing mild, the beds will begin cropping and will continue until the December frosts cause a cessation. The beds will resume cropping as soon as the weather becomes mild again in March. If artificial heat is available, then the beds will continue bearing during winter and more compost should be prepared to take over in April. There will thus be only a few weeks in the year when there will be no mushrooms. The commercial grower, with possibly three houses, will so arrange his composting that there will be no break in the supply.

Before making up the boxes, the spawn should be obtained, so that no time is lost in spawning when once the boxes are filled. One carton will spawn an area of about 40 sq. ft. Use dry, pure culture spawn which will keep almost indefinitely, and is easier to manage than moist or grain spawn.

If the boxes were treated with wood preservative (or disinfectant if they had previously borne a crop) when the compost heap was first made up, they will have become weathered by the time the compost is ready to use and they should be stacked before filling in the manner shown in Fig. 2. It will be found that a brick stood on end will give the correct support if placed between the ends of the boxes. There will be approximately 8–9 in. between the boxes which will permit picking to be done without difficulty, and will allow the boxes to be tended. Make the boxes quite secure before filling them.

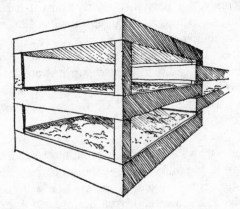

Fig. 4

Boxes supported by bricks stood on end to allow adequate space for picking and tending the mushrooms.

As soon as the compost is ready, lose no time in filling the boxes. Shake out the compost and place sufficient in each for it to reach just above the sides of the boxes. When this has

47

been done, use a brick or a piece of heavy wood to press down the compost, making it as compact as possible and paying particular attention to ensure that it is so in the corners. Then, to each box, add more compost, pressing it down again until level with the sides. Pressing down the compost is most important, for in boxes it will be found to dry out more quickly than when made up into beds on the ground. The greater the depth and the larger the box, the less rapidly will it dry out. If the compost has been correctly prepared it will be springy and will retain its heat for several days after spawning, which will ensure the spawn getting away to a good start.

When growing a few boxes at home, spawning may be done almost at once, for only in properly constructed and controlled mushroom houses is it possible to raise the temperature of the surrounding air to 130° F (54·5° C) for pasteurisation to take place. This is described in a later chapter. Nor is there need to use a hot-bed thermometer, for it is unlikely that the compost will hold a temperature above that which would harm the spawn, i.e. 70° F (21° C), for any length of time.

Spawning
Pure culture spawn is obtainable from most sundries' stores or direct from the makers and it should be purchased some days before it is to be used. When dried, it will keep almost indefinitely. The spawn is broken up into a tray or dish for easy handling, breaking it into pieces about the size of a walnut, though every portion can be used, even the dust. Spawn is greyish-white in appearance and will leave no stains on the hands, though rubber gloves may be used for spawning the compost. This is done by pressing the pieces into the compost to a depth of 1 in. and covering the inserted spawn with displaced compost. It is important that the compost is

48

in contact with the spawn, and that there are no air spaces, for the spawn can grow only when in direct contact with the composted straw, along which it runs.

The spawn should be inserted at intervals of 5–6 in. so that it will permeate every part of the compost as quickly as possible. Spawn is the most inexpensive part of a mushroom crop, costing only 10p for a box which could be expected to yield mushrooms to the value of at least £5, so it should not be used sparingly.

After the spawn has been inserted, the compost should again be pressed down firmly, and the surface made level to enable the casing or covering material to be kept at a constant thickness. If applied either too thickly or too thinly, it will affect the crop.

To prevent the top of the compost from drying out, it will be advisable to place over it thick newspapers made damp; black polythene sheeting could also be used. This will also help to exclude direct sunlight and will create the conditions of humidity the growing spawn enjoys. Never water the compost directly, for if excess moisture percolates to the spawn, it may cause it to die back.

If the boxes are stacked outside against a wall, hessian or plastic sheeting should be draped over them to maintain humidity and exclude strong winds.

After about three weeks, if the air temperature has not fallen below 50° F (10° C), the spawn will be seen to have started to grow out into the surrounding compost, which will have become a mass of greyish-white threads of mycelium. It will mean that a heavy crop is almost assured, and it will now be time to apply the casing, or covering, which is necessary to support the growing mushrooms. Into this casing material the spawn threads fuse together to form the fruiting body, the mushroom.

49

For the home grower, a mixture of horticultural peat made moist, and sterilized loam, preferably from virgin pasture-land, is suitable. These materials are obtainable from most nursery growers or garden sundries' stores, but should be ordered when the boxes are first spawned so that they will be on hand when required. They should be used at the rate of half and half by bulk, mixing them well together, but the peat should first be thoroughly moist; like straw, it will take up a considerable quantity of moisture.

It is of the greatest importance to obtain freshly sterilized loam, and this should not be allowed to become contaminated by disease spores before it is used, otherwise it may cause an outbreak of bubbles disease (*Mycogone perniciosa*). This is a disease which all growers dread, but which can be prevented by maintaining the casing materials in clean condition.

The mixture should be spread over the compost to a depth of 1½ in., no more, no less, and this may be done by using a wooden inch-ruler which is pressed into the casing every so often. The compost will have sunk 1½ in. below the top of the boxes and the casing should be made level with the top upon completion. A bucketful of soil and peat will be sufficient to case a box of about 5–6 sq. ft.

It should be said that any small stones need not be removed from the soil, nor should it be of too fine a texture, otherwise when made moist it will tend to 'pan' and form a crust, thus cutting off air from the growing spawn. A friable compost and a friable casing soil is the secret of success. Neither should the soil ever be allowed to become too wet. At all times keep it just moist, for any water seeping through to the compost below may kill off the spawn. A gentle syringing whenever the surface appears dry is all that is required, until the first pin-head mushrooms are seen. This will be about three weeks after the casing has been applied, or six weeks from the time the boxes were spawned.

The first tiny mushrooms will show above the place in which the spawn pieces were originally planted and, as the mycelium spreads, they will appear over all parts of the box. Now will be the time to give a little extra moisture, but always err on the side of dryness. The spawn will not be damaged by dryness, only retarded, but it will be by excessive moisture. However, as mushrooms have a large moisture content it is necessary for them to obtain sufficient moisture as they reach maturity. This will take seven to eight days in a temperature of 55° F (13° C) from the time when the first pin-heads are seen.

Mushrooms grow in clumps, as many as five or six or more, growing from a main base or trunk, and will appear in flushes, at intervals of ten days rather than continuously. They are removed as they reach maturity by gently twisting them away at the base, and leaving behind those still small to continue growing. Later they will appear in clusters, and also as odd mushrooms, which are removed by the same twisting action and with the roots attached. Where the mushrooms have been removed from a large base, this should be lifted out with a knife and the hole filled in without delay, using fresh sterilized soil. The surrounding spawn will at once begin to grow into it. This procedure should continue throughout the life of the crop which may be of three to four months' duration, depending upon how well the compost has been prepared.

When the crop has ended, the boxes are emptied and the compost removed to the garden. The boxes are then sterilized by soaking them with SterIzal or formaldehyde solution, and allowed to 'weather' for several weeks before being used again.

To keep the crop free from pests during cropping, the boxes should be dusted with pyrethrum powder every two to three weeks. Again, this is inexpensive and will insure trouble free mushrooms.

It may be possible to prolong the crop by watering during the last three weeks or so with a dilute solution of common salt. This is often used by farmers to increase the yield of field grown mushrooms; the land is dressed with salt where mushrooms are known to appear in autumn.

Small packs in the home

Small quantities of grain or manure spawn are obtainable from several seed houses and garden centres. A bag of spawn sufficient to spawn 50 sq. ft. costs about £1. Supplies can be obtained from Samuel Dobie Ltd. of Llangollen, N. Wales, who also market the Tubby pack for home growers. It is an ordinary plastic bucket filled with specially prepared compost and planted with spawn which has run through the compost and into the casing. The packs, which weigh about 12 lb., can be placed in a cellar, shed or beneath the kitchen sink. Remove the cover and give just sufficient water to make the casing slightly moist. Too much water will kill the spawn. Keep the pack away from sunlight, preferably in a dark place. In a temperature of 58–60° F (15–16° C), mushrooms will appear in about three weeks and continue for between eight and ten weeks. Don't worry if the temperature falls, even to freezing, for as soon as it rises to 50° F (10° C) mushrooms will soon re-appear. After cropping, use the compost on the garden and the bucket in the kitchen.

3—Scientific crop production

The scientific mushroom house—ventilation—heating—use of cement—the composting ground—sterilisation of soil—tools of the trade

If the home cultivation of mushrooms has proved successful, the grower may wish to expand into commercial production, beginning maybe with one small scientifically designed house and gradually increasing the area.

William Robinson, in his book *Mushroom Culture; its Extension and Improvement*, tells us that the first commercial mushroom house erected in this country was built for a Mr. Mundy in his garden at Shipley, near Derby, at the beginning of the nineteenth century. The design, which is still common practice 180 years later was introduced from Russia by a Mr. Oldacre, who described it in the Horticultural Society's Transactions. The house was of the lean-to type, 10 ft. wide. This allowed wooden shelf beds to be erected on either side which were $3\frac{1}{2}$ ft. wide, thus allowing 3 ft. for a central path. The house was heated by hot-water pipes through a double flue let into the pathway, and over which it was possible to walk by means of an iron grill. The modern mushroom house has been altered but little, though it has been brought up to date with the introduction of electrically operated ventilation fans and air extractors, and by the use of fibre-glass and other modern materials for insulation purposes.

Now that the use of soil for covering the beds has generally been discontinued by commercial growers, it matters little where the mushroom farm is to be set up, provided there is space for several houses, each capable of accommodating 1,000 sq. ft. of mushroom beds, and sufficient room for the preparation of the compost and the emptying of the houses without contaminating the fresh compost.

One of the most important factors in successful mushroom growing is pasteurisation of the compost as it is made up into beds. This is what is known as 'peak-heating', and Dr. Lambert discovered in the 1930s that if the house or room in which the beds were made could be subjected to a heat of between 120° and 140° F (49° and 60° C) this would not only 'sweeten' the compost, but would absorb any excess moisture from the beds. Pests and disease spores would also be eliminated. This means that the mushroom house or room must be made airtight, whilst the heating system must be capable of attaining such high temperatures.

As floor beds prove difficult to bring to such high temperatures, and in any case it is not economical to have beds only on the floor in the specially constructed mushroom house, the mushrooms are grown either in tiers or shelves, or in boxes stacked one upon another. In any case, the more compost there is in a house will enable a greater amount of heat to be generated by the compost, and there will be less difficulty in bringing the beds to the necessary high temperature with the use of artificial heat.

Well-constructed stone buildings will be capable of pasteurisation, whilst a specially constructed mushroom house will be even more satisfactory. This is the reason why it is necessary, when taking up mushroom cultivation on a commercial scale, to be provided with the correct growing conditions. It does not, however, mean that good crops cannot be grown without pasteurisation. They can. But with it, better and more reliable crops will be the result, and where growing commercially everything should be done to attain these results.

The scientific mushroom house
Where erecting new mushroom houses it will be essential to ensure that either the land may be purchased outright or that a long lease, if necessary, will be granted. And remember that before any permanent buildings are to be erected, permission must be obtained from the local Planning Authority, and detailed plans submitted.

The new mushroom house marketed by Arundel Plastics Ltd. of Beaconsfield, Bucks., has proved capable of producing heavy crops whilst enabling standards of the utmost cleanliness to be maintained. The houses are supplied in any width from 14 ft. to 28 ft. and any length from 40 ft. to 200 ft. The height is 10 ft. from the base which should be of concrete for cleanliness. The house is supplied in kit form and can be erected by two people. The frame is of galvanised steel tubing and is erected over steel foundation tubes with key clamps holding the frame together. The house is covered by Filmtex plastic sheeting which is eight times stronger than polythene. It has high storm resistance and withstands temperatures ranging from $-58°$ F to $+158°$ F ($-50°$ C to $+70°$ C). The house is insulated (between the two Filmtex sheets) with Crown 75 fibreglass to a thickness of 120 mm. Filmtex is available in white, dark green, black, grey and pewter. Either of the last two colours are most suitable for mushroom culture as they offer diffused light for the mushrooms, yet sufficient light for cultural operations to be carried out.

Concrete floors will make for cleanliness, but if capital is limited floors may be made of compressed ashes. Where boxes or trays are being used instead of tier beds, a floor composed of ashes may be topped up with fresh material after each crop, and this will prove adequate if the walls and floor have been treated with a steriliser following the removal of the boxes. Concrete is, however, superior in every way.

The boxes, which should be of stout timber and which are obtainable from fish merchants at Hull or Grimsby, will each accommodate 5 or 6 sq. ft. of compost. Boxes made of $\frac{3}{4}$-in. timber may be constructed on the premises and, if correctly handled, they will have a life of at least ten years.

Recent experiments carried out with boxes of larger size, in this instance of 25 sq. ft., have produced proportionately larger crops than the smaller sized boxes. The larger boxes have yielded $2\frac{1}{2}$–3 lb. per sq. ft. after only one month of bearing, compared with less than half that yield with boxes of 5 sq. ft. The boxes have produced progressively larger crops as size of box increased. This may be accounted for by the fact that the larger boxes are better able to retain the correct moisture content, and the compost is also able to hold its temperature longer, thus enabling the spawn to permeate the compost more strongly before adverse elements begin to make their presence felt. Boxes of a size larger than 6 sq. ft. are suitable for use only where experienced labour is available.

Where erecting staging for tier beds, the supports throughout should be of 4-in.×3-in. timber, which has been treated with Cuprinol. The beds or cross boards should be of 4-in.× 1-in. timber, which has also been treated, and which are placed about $1\frac{3}{4}$ ft. apart. Over the cross boards, asbestos or flat iron sheeting is fixed, on which the compost is placed. The life of the iron sheeting will be prolonged if treated with Jettolite bituminous coating. Only new timber should be used, but the sheets may be of second-hand material cut to the required width. Corrugated sheeting may be used as an alternative to the flat iron, but it is not advisable to bed the compost directly on to the cross boards, for they would quickly decay and would be expensive to replace. Whatever material is used to contain the compost, it must be strong, for it will have to support a considerable weight when once the beds are cased.

The side boards need not be more than 6 in. deep (wide) and some growers dispense with them altogether by sloping the sides of the beds. At least 1½ ft. should be allowed between each tier, otherwise there will be difficulty in attending to the beds and gathering the mushrooms.

Excellent mushrooms may also be grown in the Portable Concrete Buildings, manufactured by the firm of the same name, who have their premises at Adderbury East, near Banbury. Their garages, in what is known as 'battery', or semi-detached form, will be ideal for mushrooms, provided both the roof and the walls are lined and insulated.

Sheds, constructed of stout timber which has been treated with preservative, also make valuable mushroom houses, but they, too, should be lined and insulated. Or more permanent houses may be constructed of breeze blocks or of brick, in which case the walls may not need lining.

Where using more permanent materials it will be more economical to erect a house capable of accommodating about 2,000 sq. ft. of beds, and there will be a considerable saving if a double house is erected, whereby it is possible to dispense with one wall. But I must confess to having a preference for the smaller house which will be easier to fill at one time, whilst if there should happen to be an outbreak of disease or an attack from pests, only limited damage will result. With my first mushroom houses I found that if strict precautions were taken, it was rare for trouble to be carried from one room to another.

Ventilation

Remembering the need for adequate fresh air, whatever type of scientific house is to be used for mushrooms, an efficient ventilating system must be provided. One may begin by having floor ventilators made at the end of each house, whilst above the door, at either end, the Vent-Axia air extraction system should be installed, one ventilator introducing fresh air whilst the other removes the stale air. Several ventilators of the cowl-type should also be fixed to the roof at regular intervals. Remember that a 2 per cent concentration of carbon dioxide will prevent the proper development of the mushrooms.

Those flap-type ventilators which open and close from inside the house by means of a cord are not recommended, for they will allow cold air to enter the house when one may not be present, and this will often be accompanied by a sudden fall in temperature, to the detriment of the crop.

A Tornado fan will also be required to circulate the air when pasteurising, though these advanced forms of air extraction and movement are only possible where there is a supply of electricity, and there is a sufficiently large area being grown to warrant their use. The Tornado fan will also be valuable if placed halfway down the house and used during warm weather to circulate the air in conjunction with the extractor fan. The 16-in. Tornado fan, which has a speed range of 1,600 rev. per minute, is able to displace 3,000 cu. ft. of air per minute.

Heating

There will be a greater economy of fuel if two houses, or more, can be heated from the same boiler, whether it is fired by gas, oil, coke or electricity, though the installation of hot-water pipes will be more expensive than that of electric tubular heating.

Heating by hot-water pipes will make for a more humid heat than would be the case if electricity was used, which is an important factor in growing mushrooms, and though a coke-fired boiler will prove as effective as oil, gas or electricity, it will require considerably more attention. An oil or gas burner, thermostatically controlled at the required temperature, will need no attention whatsoever either by day or by night, whilst there will be no laborious handling of coke and clinker. Oil or gas heating, however, will only be economical where it is used to heat several thousand square feet of bed area.

Where using a coke-fired boiler, it is important to have the boiler considerably larger than actually necessary to heat the length of piping installed. This will allow for heating additional houses which may be added at a later date, whilst it will also be possible to raise the temperature of the house to the 140° F (60° C) which is required for pasteurisation. The use of a large boiler will also act as a safeguard during severe weather, when the coke may burn through before the boiler can be given attention, resulting in a drop in temperature and possibly the freezing up of the pipes.

A small mushroom house may be heated by electricity, or even by paraffin oil. An electric heating system controlled by a thermostat will require almost no attention, whilst most of the modern paraffin-oil heaters require filling only twice each week. Where electricity is being used it creates a dry atmosphere, and it will be necessary to damp down the house more frequently to produce the humid atmosphere enjoyed by the mushrooms. A paraffin-oil heater of the hot-water radiator type will provide the correct humidity, but the wicks must be kept scrupulously clean if the heater is not to emit fumes which will be adverse to the growing mushrooms.

Ekco Thermotubes, simple to fix, will prove most efficient, likewise the Humex tubular heater, both of which are waterproof. They should be fixed to the wall about 9 in. above floor level to allow for cleaning beneath the tubes. Humex tubular heaters have a loading of 60 watts per foot of tube and can be fitted singly or in twos. The tubes are obtainable in up to 12-ft. lengths. Ekco Thermotubes are also made of rustproof aluminium and are available in lengths up to 8 ft. Fan heaters are equally effective: the Autoheat 3000 manufactured by Findlay, Irvine Ltd. has a built-in thermometer and temperature-control knob. To assist with regulation of fan speed, an A.C. regulator enables the fan to be worked at four different speeds. Automatic heat control is necessary to maintain the right temperature for spawn growth and a dripproof thermostat is obtainable from manufacturers of heating equipment.

Where pasteurisation is to be carried out and where high temperatures are required to ensure a rapid spawn 'run', what is known as 'gilled' tubular pipes, for use with a steam or hot-water boiler, may be installed. The pipes should be placed on that part of the floor of the house above which the trays or tiers are placed. The tubing may readily be uncoupled and moved to another house for pasteurisation purposes.

The Baxi Hot Air stove brings quite a new method of heating to the mushroom house. Instead of heating water pipes in the conventional way, it heats the air of the house to a high temperature. The moment the fire in the boiler is lighted, heated air begins to circulate through ducting directed to all parts of the house. There are no expensive hot-water pipes to install, yet the stove is equally efficient. No. 3 stove has a heating capacity of more than 20,000 cu. ft.

In paraffin-oil heaters the Stourbridge single-pipe heater—

the pipe is supplied to the required length of the house—will burn for 48 hours on 1 gallon of paraffin oil, and if one stove and pipe is provided on both sides of a house it will maintain a steady heat, though where using this method of heating it will not be possible to carry out pasteurisation.

Bryant's '666' hot-water radiator, with adjustable hot-air pipes, the Eltex Blue-Flame and Aladdin paraffin oil heaters, and Rowland Spencer's oil-fired heaters are most efficient. There are also various gas heaters suitable for mushroom growing and Thermal Tempest Engineering of Yaxley and Cooper-Walker of Edinburgh make several which do not need manual control.

Use of cement

Where there is a cement floor this is a considerable advantage, and is greatly to be preferred to the solid earth floor of rhubarb houses, greenhouses and caves, which quickly become contaminated by diseases that often prove difficult to eradicate. This is why stable blocks, old cotton mills, breweries and warehouses are so valuable for mushroom growing, whilst army and Royal Air Force huts, which have served their purpose, will also prove suitable, for they, too, will usually have a concrete floor.

Contamination of the earth floor of the caves around Paris was described by Robinson who wrote: 'After a time the great quarries (caves) seem to become tired of their occupants or the mushrooms dislike the air. They are then cleaned out, the very soil where the beds rested being scraped away and the place left to recruit itself for a year or two.'

The same operation is also necessary where growing on an earth floor today, though the use of formaldehyde to wash down the house and soak the floor will provide complete sterilisation. Growers, however, did not know this until the late 1930s, when this form of sterilisation removed entirely the adverse effects of site contamination which previously caused trouble, even where a concrete floor was used, though to a less extent.

Where growing mushrooms on a commercial scale, and where large sums may have been invested, it is essential that everything be done to safeguard the crop. Cleanliness is the first essential in the production of a profitable crop. Wherever possible, the mushroom house should have a concrete floor, whilst for the same reason the ground where the compost is cured should also have a concrete base, to enable it to be washed down after each heap of compost has been prepared and removed to the mushroom house.

At the end of the stable block in which I grew my first mushrooms was a concrete turning ground, large enough to accommodate ten tons of manure, and to permit its turning. Such a quantity will be sufficient to make up 1,000 sq. ft. of bed area. The ground possessed a slight slope from which any surplus moisture could drain whilst the manure (or straw where a synthetic compost is being prepared) was being watered upon delivery.

Used compost removed from the beds should never come into contact with the ground on which fresh compost is to be prepared for fear of contamination and so, with my first venture into mushroom cultivation, a small area of ground was reserved at the other side of the building to accommodate the used compost. This suggestion should be followed wherever mushrooms are being grown, and whilst the high cost of labour demands that the compost should not be conveyed long distances, it will help to keep down pest and disease attack if these instructions are carried out when the crop has finished. Strict cleanliness is essential at all times when growing mushrooms. Where using a building, or a piece of land for mushroom cultivation on a commercial scale, space will be required both to prepare and remove the compost.

A good road is also essential for the delivery and removal of the manure. Here again I was fortunate, in that leading to my stable block was a drive of sufficient width to accommodate a large lorry. An excellent entrance way may be constructed from crushed brick and rubble removed from a property which is being demolished. The rubble should be made as firm as possible, for it should be remembered that it will have to take the weight of several tons at a time, and it will be almost impossible to make deliveries during wet weather where there is not a suitable roadway. The need for making a roadway may be overcome if the site is situated close to a main road, and the manure may be thrown from the lorry directly on to the turning ground.

The composting ground
The composting site may be protected from heavy rains by the erection of a roof, which may be of corrugated iron, asbestos or bitumen felt supported on stout posts. It should, however, be at least 10 ft. from ground level and 3–4 ft. above the top of the compost heap, otherwise the steam from the compost will cause condensation on the roof. This will fall on to the manure, thereby causing the upper portion to become too wet. An open barn with a high roof will be more suitable, provided it has a concrete floor, or the compost may be prepared without any protection, provided the heap is made tall and left rounded at the top. It may also be given protection by covering with straw.

It is advisable, however, to provide the composting site with some protection from prevailing winds if the situation is exposed. Wattle hurdles, or preferably interwoven fencing, erected against the prevailing wind, will do much to prevent the compost from becoming too dry. For the same reason a large heap may be more uniformly prepared than a small heap, into which strong winds can blow and cause drying and burning.

A reliable water supply is essential, for with the preparation of the compost, cleaning down the house and watering the beds, large quantities will be required. Water may be pumped from a stream or well by means of an Argosy pumping set, complete with its petrol engine or electric motor. It will pump for a distance of 100 ft., and will be capable of pumping at a rate of nearly 500 gallons per hour, which should be sufficient to meet all one's requirements. These pumps are indispensable where mains water is not available, but mains should be brought to the site wherever possible, for it has untold advantages over pumping one's own supply.

Electricity is a great saving of labour. It may be used for pumping water, for air circulation, and for heating the houses and for lighting. Today there are few areas without electricity, and if not already connected to the site it is usually not a difficult matter to have it installed as soon as the buildings are ready. Should the supply fail at any time due to power cuts or breakdowns, the beds will not be harmed, though production may be retarded.

Sterilisation of soil

The experienced grower now uses a mixture of peat and chalk for casing the beds and no soil is ever brought onto the mushroom establishment. Many growers, however, still use soil, and though not absolutely essential, where growing on a commercial scale a supply should be on hand, otherwise it will be necessary to transport all that is required for covering (casing) the beds. A ton of soil will be needed to case beds of an area of about 1,000 sq. ft. and to a depth of 1½ in., whilst about half that quantity will be required to fill in the holes which are left when the mushrooms have been removed.

Where soil is used it should be sterilised, having first been obtained from pasture which has not been contaminated by the compost removed from old beds. There are various methods of sterilisation, which are described in Chapter 9, but sufficient room should be available to carry out the work. Sterilised soil may be obtained from a local nurseryman who may have an efficient sterilising plant, and who may be pleased to supply one's requirements for a reasonable charge in order to reduce his own overheads. However, where growing mushrooms as a livelihood, it will be advisable to purchase a small sterilising outfit at a cost of about £10, though a home-made contraption of reasonable efficiency may be made as an alternative.

For a grower of up to 2,000 sq. ft. of bed area the Autosoil electric steriliser is most efficient. It is automatic, switching itself off after sterilisation has been completed. It will sterilise a bushel of soil at one time, and by using the machine over several days sufficient soil may be sterilised to case 1,000 sq. ft. of bed. The steriliser is marketed by S.E.S. Ltd., Westfields Road, London, W.3 at a reasonable price; it is also available on hire purchase. The serious grower should most certainly invest in one and safeguard his crops, until he becomes proficient in the use of peat and chalk, for diseases of the soil can wipe out in a few days the most promising crops.

Tools of the trade
Where growing on a large scale, a packing-shed, or room fitted with benches, and preferably attached to the growing block, will be an essential. Here the mushrooms will be cleaned (if necessary), weighed and placed in baskets, or pun-

nets, ready for transporting to market. The packing-room should be as cool as possible, but should have plenty of light, for here the booking and writing up of all information appertaining to the crop should be attended to. Here, too, should be kept those more important tools of the trade, i.e., a hot-bed thermometer and a soil-and-manure-testing outfit, insecticides, a pair of reliable scales, and the necessary packing materials. The only other tool of importance is a manure fork.

Some form of transport will be required where consigning large quantities of mushrooms to market. If they are to be sent by rail it may be possible to arrange with the British Railway authorities to collect at one's mushroom farm at such a time as to make allowance for the various rail connections, and so that the produce reaches the market at a time most suitable to the wholesaler.

4—Obtaining the manure

Food value of manure—why compost?—obtaining supplies—making the stack

Large-scale mushroom production demands large supplies of manure, and the most economic and satisfactory is horse manure which is still obtainable from racing and riding stables situated in most populated parts of the British Isles. As William Robinson wrote a century ago: 'the fresher the manure is, the longer the crop will last. Every gardener who makes up beds with unheated droppings knows how superior they are to fermented manure.' Manure obtained from grain- or bran-fed horses, bedded with wheat straw, will retain its heat for some time, and will not become sticky in the beds as will manure from horses fed on roots and silage. Greasy manure will set like lard in the beds and will rapidly lose heat, and must be avoided.

The straw is of great importance. It should be wheat straw, for oat and barley straw break down too rapidly in the heap and will tend to make the manure greasy, whilst rye straw proves difficult to break down at all. On straw there is a calose on which the growing spawn runs, feeding on the cellulose and lignin which is stored in the straw. In 1928 Falck, in Germany, had discovered that these valuable foods were reduced in strength (food value) as the manure is composted. About the same time Treschow, in Poland, had reported getting a heavy growth of mycelium on a substance known as xylose. This is a form of carbohydrate which is present as xylan only in wheat straw. It therefore stands to reason that only manure made up of wheat straw should be used in the preparation of a mushroom compost.

It is also important that the straw is saturated with urine and that the manure has a strong smell of ammonia. Straw lacking in urine will never grow a heavy crop and when making up a synthetic compost, the preparation called urea or other substitutes should be used to replace the urine. From wherever one's manure supplies are to be obtained, it is important that the manure is as fresh as possible. Manure stored for a considerable time may have become over-composted in the heap, whilst heavy rains may have washed out much of the valuable urine where stored in the open.

Again, if stored under cover, or for a lengthy period in a large heap, and possibly if the straw is too dry, 'burning' may take place. This is known as fire-fang, and is denoted by the appearance of whitish-grey patches in the manure. It is caused by anaerobic heating, and besides destroying valuable plant foods where it is excessive, prolonged heating at a high temperature may cause a disease known as chae-tomium to appear, which will later destroy the spawn in the beds. There is no known cure for this so it must be prevented.

Both the straw and the droppings supply the spawn with its food. About half the nitrogen requirements come from the droppings, provided by the urine in the straw. Protein, from which the mushroom obtains its supplies of phosphorus, is provided by the droppings, whilst potassium salts are also present in straw which is saturated with urine. The necessary calcium, so often lacking in manure, is added in the form of gypsum (calcium sulphate).

The droppings are also necessary to generate sufficient heat to bring the straw into a suitable condition to produce the maximum crop. The manure should, therefore, contain only as many droppings as necessary for the correct composting of the straw, a proportion of 1 part droppings to 3 parts straw saturated in urine being the ideal. Too many droppings will cause the compost to become too compact, thus depriving it of the necessary air needed to bring about bacterial activity, or what is known as aerobic fermentation. Manure which appears to contain too many droppings should have additional moist straw incorporated, so as to lighten the heap and to prevent a greasy compost. Where straw saturated in urine can be obtained, so much the better, but failing this, clean wheat straw should be saturated with water before it is added to the heap. If sufficient moisture is not given, the fresh straw will burn and, whilst lightening the heap, it will provide little in the way of food for the mycelium. Cow manure should never be used, for it will not provide sufficient heat, and quickly becomes cold and greasy when in the beds. The droppings from other animals may be used and these will be described in a later chapter on synthetic composting.

Today, where horse manure is in short supply, straw which has been partially composted by treating with urea or with sulphate of ammonia, may be added to the heap. This will partially break down the straw, in addition to providing valuable extra nitrogen to help in the composting of any straw in the manure which has not received sufficient urine. The straw should be treated by first making it thoroughly moist, and then adding the sulphate of ammonia as it is being formed into a heap. It is turned and shaken out after about six days, and in another four to five days will be ready to add to the manure. The straw throughout will then be in a similar condition to begin composting.

It may be that manure containing an excess of long straw

and few droppings will not contain sufficient nitrogen for its correct composting. The nitrogen content of the stack on a dry weight basis may be less than 1·5 per cent whilst the nitrogen content at the time the beds are filled should be 2·25 per cent. Manure which is made up of the correct amount by weight of straw, urine and droppings will ensure that the nitrogen content will be achieved during the preparation of the compost and by the time the manure is ready for spawning. But not all composts contain sufficient nitrogen to produce a maximum crop, and where the straw is long and dry (urine being absent) and droppings are scarce, it is advisable to incorporate at the first turn or when the heap is first made up, a small quantity—14 lb. per ton of manure—of an activator with a high nitrogen content and one which contains the most readily available nitrogen. The nitrogen content of Adco 'M' and cotton seed meal (mostly used in America) is about 7 per cent whilst that of brewer's grain meal is about half that content. At Darlington's Experimental Farm, 28 lb. of cotton seed meal was at one time added to each ton of manure at the first turn with worthwhile results.

The nitrogen content of manure may be laboratory tested, and Darlingtons, now Darmycel Ltd., of Rustington, Sussex, will make a detailed analysis upon receipt of a sample taken from the heap just prior to the first turn, and again just before the compost is ready for spawning. Sufficient samples of compost should be taken from different sections of the heap at regular spacings apart to fill a cardboard box of about 12 cu. in. The compost should be well mixed before it is placed in the box so as to provide a fair sample of the whole heap.

Why compost?
Enthusiasts may wish to know why it is necessary to compost

at all? It is, of course, important to make the manure into as rich a source of food for the spawn as possible, and mushrooms require nitrates, potash, calcium and phosphates, just like any other plants. It must be remembered that, possessing no green colouring matter, the mushroom must obtain all its requirements from the growing medium, it cannot take them from the atmosphere.

It is also essential that the compost is neither too alkaline nor too acid when it is spawned, for an excess in either respect will result in failure. Also, it is necessary for the compost to have attained peak temperatures before being spawned. Should the compost heat up to a temperature above 75° F (24° C) after it is spawned, the mycelium may be killed.

Upon the successful preparation of the compost, therefore, depends the profitability of the crop, and the experienced grower is able to prepare a satisfactory compost, just as the experienced cook can make a cake; failure is never contemplated. When such confidence has been achieved, one may go ahead without thought of failure.

Until Pizer's investigations with the use of gypsum, large crops had never been enjoyed, and its introduction was the turning point in commercial mushroom production. The novice grower, too, who wishes to put down a small mushroom bed in a barn or possibly beneath the greenhouse bench, will obtain much heavier crops if gypsum is used in the preparation of the compost, quite apart from its ability to prevent a greasy compost. It may be said that the use of gypsum is the secret of success in mushroom growing.

When the manure arrives and is quite fresh, it will give off a strong smell of ammonia. This smell will gradually disappear, as the ammonia is converted into protein. The use of gypsum will help to prevent any loss of nitrogen in the ammonia whilst being given off in the gas form as it is being

71

converted. If urine is not present in the manure in sufficient quantity, the nitrogen, necessary to enable bacterial action in the heap to take place so as to break down the various substances into plant food, will be lacking. This may be partially overcome by saturating a quantity of wheat straw with a solution of ammonium sulphate. Or dried blood (in liquid form) may be used to provide the necessary nitrogen. If there is no smell of ammonia, either the manure has been composted too far whilst collected and stored, in which case it will have a black appearance and should be rejected, or it will not contain sufficient urine, and this must be rectified before composting begins.

The aim is, therefore, to employ the various ingredients already present in the manure, or which have been added in such a way that they will best be converted into plant food, whilst at the same time the physical condition of the compost is improved.

Where only limited supplies of horse manure can be obtained, or where the straw appears unduly long and dry and lacking urine, the straw may be removed and mixed with additional straw which has been partially composted with a synthetic preparation such as Adco 'M'. After several days in the heap the straw may then be added to the manure and prepared in the normal way. This method is particularly useful where there is a larger proportion of droppings than advisable. As previously stated, straw may also be treated with urea or ammonium sulphate to assist with its composting. Manure containing too little straw in proportion to the droppings will prevent correct fermentation and cause the manure to become sticky. At the same time the compost will not be converted into material which contains the food required to produce a heavy crop of mushrooms.

Obtaining the manure

Obtaining supplies

Where obtaining horse manure, which is the best material yet discovered for mushroom growing, a visit should be made to the supplier, whether it be a riding school or a racing establishment, and should any other material be used for bedding purposes, such as sawdust, peat moss or maybe another type of straw, it should be possible to persuade the owner to change the bedding to wheat straw if one is prepared to pay the difference in price for the manure. Wheat straw is the first essential in the preparation of a satisfactory compost for mushrooms.

One should also obtain the manure in as fresh a condition as possible, for then there will be little fear that the manure will have become too wet and over-composted, or may have become burnt through anaerobic heating should the straw be too dry, due possibly to having been kept in the heap for too long a period. I think it was because of these considerations that the old growers suggested using the manure in the fresh condition, for to store for too long will usually prove detrimental, and over-composted manure will never produce a big crop. At the same time, to spawn manure which is in a too fresh condition will mean that the complex substances which it contains will not have been fully converted into food capable of producing the maximum crop. Somehow one has to strike the happy medium, and this is the problem the beginner has to face—the manure must be neither over- nor under-composted.

If only small quantities of manure are to be composted at one time, try to persuade the supplier to save the approximate amount for delivery or collection on the required date, so that the quantity required will not be contaminated with older manure, which would make it difficult to bring all the com-

73

post to the necessary condition. If the manure can be stored under cover, so much the better, for straw which is saturated with urine will generally contain sufficient moisture for its preparation, and if exposed to heavy rains may take some time to dry. Unduly wet manure will fail to heat up correctly, and there will not be sufficient bacterial activity to convert the ingredients in the manure into suitable plant food.

Manure which has been stored for too long and which will not heat up correctly, will be troubled by pests and diseases, even if it should produce a crop. Styer has reported that spores of brown plaster mould are killed at a temperature of 126° F (50° C), and as the disease is usually troublesome in a sticky, wet compost which may not at any stage have achieved so high a temperature, it is vital that, if only to eliminate this disease, wet, over-composted manure should be avoided. Also, manure in this condition will be too alkaline when ready for spawning, with the result that the equally dreaded white plaster mould may make its appearance. The old growers were, therefore, quite correct in believing that fresh, under-composted manure is preferable to manure which has been over-composted and which may be well on the way to that state when delivered.

Pests may also not be destroyed, should the compost not heat correctly. Where this has not taken place, nematodes or eel-worms will cause havoc. If the compost has attained a heat of 145° F (68° C) for 48 hours they will be entirely destroyed, but should they remain in the compost, they will devour the food required by the mycelium, thus preventing further growth and reducing the compost to an inert black mass. Few mushrooms will be seen.

Making the stack
As previously stated, the larger the heap the better will the

compost be prepared, for a small heap of manure will not attain the high temperature necessary for the elimination of all pests and diseases, whilst it will always prove more difficult to bring to the desired physical condition. Again, where the manure is to be prepared in the open, moisture from heavy rains will affect no more than the top inch or two of a large pile and the compost will not become too wet. With only a small pile, a very much larger proportion of the compost will be made moister, and this would have adverse results where the compost had perhaps reached the right condition for bedding.

Strong winds, too, will dry out a small heap of manure, making it difficult for the straw to retain sufficient moisture to ensure correct bacterial activity. Quantities of no more than a ton of manure should, therefore, be turned under cover, and where this is impractical the manure should be stacked in the corner formed by two walls and where the heap is to be turned. During wet weather a canopy placed over the top of the heap will give protection from excessive moisture as the compost is reaching maturity.

5—Preparation of the compost

When to make a start—arrival of manure—use of gypsum—additional ingredients—making the first turn—conditions in the heap—how long to compost?—testing for pH value—a valuable new activator

Before making a start on mushroom growing the beginner will be anxious to know exactly when will be the most suitable time to commence operations. This will depend entirely upon whether the building to be used can be heated to maintain production during winter, when mushrooms command top prices. If heat is available, the compost should be prepared during August, a time of year not noted for heavy rains. If the beds are made up early in September the temperature outside the house will be sufficiently high to ensure a satisfactory spawn 'run'. With gentle warmth indoors, the beds will commence to crop early in October and should continue until the end of February. One will thus be spared the excessively high temperatures of summer which cause so much trouble with pests and diseases and usually produce a mushroom of inferior quality.

Where there is no heat available a start should be made late in March, bedding down the compost at the end of April and relying on natural warmth to effect a good spawn run. The first mushrooms will be ready to gather about June 1st and the crop should continue until the end of August to make way for the winter crop in early September, if some

76

form of heating can then be provided. This may be from profits of the summer crop.

Where one is growing commercially it may be possible to divide a building into two or four separate growing-rooms or compartments, each of which could be sealed off to permit pasteurisation and fumigation. If polythene houses are used, two would provide a succession of mushrooms throughout the year, when there would be continuity in supplying one's wholesaler and an income all the year round.

The most important crops are those which bear mushrooms between November 1st and April 30th, a time when there are few choice vegetables in the garden to compete. Mushrooms, too, are always most appreciated when there is an R in the month, the time of steaks and stews. During the six months of winter and spring, top quality mushrooms retail at about £1 per lb. with wholesale prices in the region of 60p to 70p per lb.

To enjoy these remunerative prices, beds should be made up during September and again in December, when they will bear crops from October until the end of May. If house (or room) No. 1, in which the beds were spawned in September, is emptied during February and new beds made up and spawned around April 1st, there would be mushrooms from May until the end of August, and the month of September, when field mushrooms are often plentiful, left free for steri-lising the house. House No. 2 would be cleared in June and new beds made up in August to crop from the beginning of October and so on, thus providing an all-the-year-round supply when most mushrooms are at their highest prices. Where mushrooms are being grown in boxes and the spawn is to be 'run' in a room provided with especially high temperatures, to be transferred later to a cropping house, it is possible to obtain four or five crops a year, but this is for the specialist grower, not the beginner.

The months of July and August are perhaps the most difficult for the grower. Temperature and humidity are high, with the result that, if air-circulation fans and extractors are not fitted, conditions will be such that the mushrooms will grow long-stemmed and will be light in weight. Many more will be required to the pound, than those produced under cooler conditions. At this time of the year, too, there is only limited demand for mushrooms, for many people are away on holiday, whilst the mushroom has to compete with a wide range of fresh fruits and vegetables in the luxury class.

I well remember taking over a large building in the midst of several of our largest iron and steel works in Sheffield and, as the building was not heated, the manure was bedded down only in April as flat beds on the floor. This new building increased the area of mushroom beds to nearly 50,000 sq. ft., a considerable increase from the 100 sq. ft. with which I had commenced operations five years previously.

The beds, which were situated 5 miles from my farm, produced nearly 2 lb. per sq. ft., but what a headache they gave when, on a warm Bank Holiday weekend in August, and and with no demand, the beds were white all over. All doors and ventilators were opened, and blocks of ice placed around the inside walls to retard the mushrooms as much as possible. All Bank Holiday Monday afternoon and throughout the night, we gathered the crop and sent them to nearby markets in the early hours of Tuesday morning, nearly 1,000 lb., and we were extremely glad to see them away.

Sufficient manure should be obtained at one time, capable of filling at least one room of a building, or the whole of one house, having a capacity of between 1,000 and 2,000 sq. ft. The manure may have to be obtained from different sources to ensure this, but it should arrive within the same week and be of approximately the same age. If it can be collected from the same stables so much the better.

For some years it has been standard practice with many American growers to obtain their mushroom compost on contract, already prepared, which is delivered ready to make up into beds for spawning. It may be made either from animal manure or from synthetic products and will be prepared and delivered exactly when the grower requires it. In Britain and also in Holland, several firms now provide this service, which is valuable to the smaller commercial grower in that his labour will be reduced to a minimum whilst the compost, prepared by experts who have had long experience, comes in perfect condition; if growing conditions are good, it may be expected to produce a profitable crop.

Arrival of the manure
On arrival, the manure may contain broken bottles, rags, tin cans and, indeed, almost anything which comes to be thrown into the manure pit. Generally, the straw will have a dry appearance and should be made thoroughly moist. The commercial grower will use a hose-pipe which is 'played' on to the manure whilst it is being unloaded. Manure which has come a distance by rail and which may have occupied the truck for a week or more will be especially dry and will require large quantites of moisture.

It is essential that the manure be made thoroughly moist at this stage, and professional growers try to give all the moisture necessary for the entire composting period at the one time. As we have seen, moisture is necessary to commence bacterial activity and to prevent 'burning'. Growing spawn (mycelium) requires moisture in addition to food, and will make only limited headway if the compost is too dry.

It will be almost impossible to give the manure too much moisture, provided it is fresh and has the power to heat up and make use of the moisture in its composting. But should the manure arrive as a very dark brown material and with the straw 'short', it will signify that it has been kept for some little time and will be partially composted. Provided the compost has not passed its peak temperature, nor appears to have suffered from burning, it will make quite a good compost, though it will require greater care with its preparation and no additional water should be given. This is most important, for it is quite possible with manure of this type to give more moisture than it can absorb for satisfactory composting. The result will be a black, sticky compost which will quickly lose heat when made into beds, whilst it will tend to become too alkaline for vigorous mycelium growth. In place of water, gypsum should be used.

Use of gypsum

The introduction of gypsum, hydrated calcium sulphate, made it possible to prepare a compost almost entirely free from greasiness, this being due to the provision of an excess of calcium over magnesium and sodium salts which are present in all manures and where present in excess, result in a greasy compost.

Pink gypsum is to be obtained from most builders or agricultural merchants or, where large quantities are required, direct from the Gypsum Mines of Kingston-on-Soar, near Nottingham. It is most inexpensive, a ton costing only about five pounds.

Gypsum is so valuable in the preparation of a satisfactory compost that no manure should ever be prepared without it. About 28 lb. should be added to every ton of manure, approximately 20 lb. being given as the manure is being unloaded on

Preparation of the compost

the site. This will become well mixed throughout the heap and for any particularly wet areas an additional 7-8 lb. may be given later in the composting, for there is little fear of giving too much.

In addition to preventing any greasiness, gypsum opens up the compost and so improves aeration that the bacteria are able to carry out their functions from the beginning. Not only does the correct aerobic fermentation take place, thereby saving several days in the preparation of the compost, but the use of gypsum also prevents loss of protein. This will happen when an excess of nitrogen is allowed to escape with the ammonia fumes, and the quicker bacterial action can prevent this taking place so much the better, whilst any unpleasant smell will vanish without delay.

Compost which arrives in an over-moist, partially composted condition may be dried out and so composted that it can be taken into the house in a suitable condition, if gypsum has been used. There is, in fact, little chance of over-watering, for gypsum gives the manure a greater capacity for not absorbing moisture. This also encourages decomposition, and so hastens the preparation of the compost that it is now possible to prepare the manure within ten days from the first turn.

The mineral calcium, which is provided by the gypsum, is required in the mushroom's diet in addition to salts of phosphorus, potassium and iron. Gypsum has thus proved itself to be indispensable in the cultivation of mushrooms and, as has been said, there is little fear of giving an excess. However, to add more than 28 lb. per ton of manure, except possibly to dry out an over-moist area, will be wasteful.

Additional ingredients
The American growers have for long added superphosphate

of lime at the rate of 14 lb. to every ton of manure. It is also used in most synthetic composts in a similar quantity. There is, however, a chance that, where phosphorus is already present in substantial amounts in the manure, an excess may cause the crop to depreciate rather than increase. Since all manure varies slightly in its mineral content and in its physical properties, it is almost impossible to determine the exact amount of superphosphate required. Some guide may, however, be given in the composition of the manure, for where droppings are in short supply this may be taken to mean that additional phosphorus might prove beneficial. It will, however, be better to play safe and give only half the amount used by the American growers until we know more about its value.

The function of superphosphate is to promote vigorous spawn (mycelium) growth. Mushrooms will, therefore, appear more quickly and will be of better quality. An excess, however, may make the beds too acid too soon, and this will reduce the ultimate weight of the crop. The superphosphate should be added at the last turn outdoors before the manure is conveyed to the house.

Though mushrooms require potash in their diet, wheat-straw animal manure will supply most of that which is thought to be necessary. The inorganic sulphate of potash may be used in synthetic composts.

The unloading and stacking of the manure is of vital importance and, done correctly, it will enable a suitable compost to be prepared in almost half the time usually considered practical.

On a visit to Messrs. W. Darlington & Sons' mushroom farm at Angmering, in Sussex, they described how it was possible to bring the manure into a suitable condition for spawning within nine days after the first turn. But what takes place in the stack before the first turn is given is all-important.

82

Preparation of the compost

As the stack is built up the manure is saturated with water if the straw shows any appearance of dryness. The total moisture requirements are given at this time so that bacterial activity can commence at once. Gypsum is sprinkled about the manure to prevent a greasy compost, and the stack is made about 8 ft. high. It is allowed from seven to ten days to heat up and partially decompose, before the first turn is given. The key to success lies in saturated straw and, as previously mentioned, there are numerous ways of doing this. All too often, however, the manure is stacked in a dry condition when it may take several weeks to bring to the correct physical condition.

Now begins the most important part of mushroom growing, namely the turning and preparation of the manure. At first the straw will be long and matted together and, as all but the very largest growers turn by hand, it will take considerable force to pull the straw apart and shake it out. Two men with experience of this work will be able to turn about 10 tons, sufficient for 1,000 sq. ft., in one day, but the first turn will occupy the longest time.

The object is to bring every part of the heap to the required condition so that it will be capable of giving the maximum yield and in the shortest possible time. It is, therefore, important that every portion of the manure receives its quota of moisture and air to encourage bacterial or aerobic activity, in addition to the various ingredients necessary for the preparation of a satisfactory compost.

As the manure is turned (and with the first turn the ammonia fumes may affect the eyes) the droppings should be mixed with the long straw, and if any dry parts remain additional water should be given. Also, where any portions of the heap appear to be unduly moist, gypsum should be given. The work cannot be rushed, for it is most important that every part of the heap is given individual treatment and, though it is possible to delegate later turnings to others, I have always made it a point to help with the first and final turns, for no other work is of greater importance.

Making the first turn
The manure should be thoroughly shaken about, mixing in well the gypsum which was thrown into the heap as it was first built up. More water may be required here and there, and perhaps additional gypsum as the stack is rebuilt.

The measurements of the heap are important. If built too high there may be anaerobic fermentation and 'burning' will result, thus causing the manure to lose much of its food value. If not made sufficiently high, the heap may fail to reach the necessary temperature. Also, the manure will become too dry should windy weather prevail, or it may become saturated during periods of heavy rain.

Where the manure is long and strawy it will require less air to bring about its fermentation than where it is short and partially composted. The heap for the first turn should therefore be made about 6 ft. high, and this will allow the manure to become reasonably compact without trampling. The height of the heap should be slightly reduced with each succeeding turn so that at the final turn it should be made no more than 5 ft. high, otherwise the manure at the base will become 'soggy', due to lack of air. The result will be that much of the compost will be too wet when ready to make into beds.

Experiments conducted by Dr. Lambert in America led him to believe that for average manure, where the straw is neither too long nor too short, the heap should be made 6 ft. high and with a base no more than 5 ft. wide so that sufficient oxygen would be able to reach the centre of the heap. The heap may be made to any practical length, the sides being made straight for the first 4 ft. of height, and then gradually rounded to permit rainwater to run off with the least possible penetration.

For the beginner there may be difficulty in keeping the base of the heap to the correct width, and it will be an advantage to mark out the ground with either chalk or sawdust to the necessary dimensions.

Where the manure can be prepared under cover the heap should be built only 5 ft. high throughout and have a base of no more than 4–5 ft. wide. To prevent excess oxygen reaching the heap the sides should be beaten hard as the heap is built up.

Working to these dimensions will ensure that the compost is prepared in the quickest possible time, and if the total water requirements are given as the manure is unloaded it should be possible to compost within ten days of giving the first turn.

Where composting less than 1 ton, it will be better to turn the manure against a wall or under cover for strong winds may cause it to dry out, thus preventing sufficient bacterial activity. Too dry manure will not heat up and will prove difficult to convert into food suitable for growing a good crop. If it is unable to be turned against a wall the heap should be left almost square and the top covered during showery weather. The sides may be prevented from drying out if covered with sacking.

If the manure arrives in what appears to be a too wet condition it may be prevented from becoming too compact if the heap is built around a small tripod, rather like the farmers in Scotland build their corn-ricks. This will permit a greater supply of oxygen to reach the centre and base of the heap. The condition should right itself if gypsum is used and the tripod may be dispensed with at the next turn. It is not advisable to use a tripod if the manure contains an abundance

85

of long straw, for too great an inrush of air will cause 'burning'.

Professors Sinden and Hauser discovered that if the outside of the heap was trampled or beaten and made compact, where an abundance of long straw is present, this will have exactly the opposite effect to the use of a tripod and will prevent too much oxygen reaching the centre, thus retarding composting. But every heap must be treated on its merits, for with horse manure no two heaps are ever alike, and though this type of manure is still the best medium in which to grow mushrooms, perhaps when we know more about synthetic composting, heavier crops may be obtained by this method.

Conditions in the heap

Beginners will require to know exactly when to make the second turning. This should be when the temperature of the heap has stopped rising and it may be noticed that the rounded top of the heap is beginning to shrink. Only experienced growers, however, are able to tell the exact time, which will be when bacterial activity has stopped for want of more air and perhaps additional moisture, in the same way that experienced cooks can bake a good cake without weighing the ingredients or constantly opening the oven door!

A special hot-bed thermometer can be used, and if this is inserted at several places in the heap each day, the rise in the temperature will be observed. A temperature of at least 160° F (71° C) may, and in fact should, be recorded, for it is desirable that such a temperature be obtained in order that the spores of fusarium disease, brown plaster mould and other troublesome diseases are killed before introducing the manure to the house. This is of particular importance where compost in the growing-room cannot be subjected to peak heating. It is also advisable that, as the heap reaches its peak temperature and injurious pests are driven to the outside, it is sprayed with a modern insecticide so that as many pests as possible may be eliminated at this stage.

If the manure has been made sufficiently moist the temperature will begin to rise for between three and five days, at which time it will have reached a peak and will be ready for turning again so as to enable more air, and possibly moisture, to enter the heap. In this way bacterial activity may begin afresh and the compost will eventually be converted into the maximum amount of food required by the mushroom. Remember that manure which is either too moist or too dry will fail to heat up correctly, and where this is so it will take very much longer to become properly composted.

Again, no definite ruling can be given as to the exact time to make another turn. Short manure which may arrive in a partially composted condition will generally be ready to turn after three or four days, whereas very long, fresh manure may take as long as a week before it reaches its peak heat. However, as soon as the temperature begins to fall the second turn should be given.

Once again the new heap should be made up and again the manure should be shaken out thoroughly, mixing any dry portions with moist areas and possibly giving a little more water where necessary and additional gypsum to the over-moist parts, so that with each turn every part of the manure is brought into that condition most suitable for the production of a heavy crop. Make sure that the outside of the heap is turned into the centre of the new stack, so that every portion is subjected to the same high temperature at some stage of its preparation and undergoes the necessary bacterial activity. Again, do not rush the turning operation, for upon its thoroughness will depend the weight of the crop.

How long to compost?

Exactly how many turns to give will depend upon the physical condition of the manure. The amount of time between each turn should diminish, and after the second turn the manure will have entirely lost any smell of ammonia, whilst the straw will be breaking down and becoming shorter as well as taking on a richer brown colour. A third turn will be required after about three days when the compost will have lost all unpleasant smell and will have turned a rich dark brown colour. Should it still appear somewhat 'green' in colour, it will denote a greasy compost and will show that satisfactory composting has not occurred. Additional gypsum should be given and possibly another turn will be necessary to bring it into condition. Though it is usual to give about 28 lb. of gypsum to each ton of manure, the exact amount must depend upon its physical condition for, as previously said, no two loads of manure will be alike.

Exactly how many turns to give has always caused controversy amongst growers. The growers of old spawned the compost in almost a fresh condition. Robinson in his book quotes a Mr. Cuthill as saying that the manure should not be allowed to heat before it is put into the beds, 'for previously heated manure does not produce such fine mushrooms'. In contrast, Falconer, the first authority on mushroom growing in America, writing at the end of the nineteenth century, has said that it took more than three weeks to compost manure, turning every other day, which would appear to be quite unnecessary and a considerable waste of labour.

Three turns given every four days with possibly a fourth turn if the manure arrived in a 'long' condition would appear to be normal. The last turn may be given when the compost is removed to the house, and if pasteurisation cannot be done

Preparation of the compost

then it will be advisable to allow the heap to heat up indoors and to fumigate before the beds are made up. Some degree of conditioning will take place where high temperatures are reached indoors, and if the beds are then made up there will be little loss of heat and a reliable crop may be expected. Though it is important that the manure should not be spawned in a 'green' or under-composted condition, it is even more important that it is not over-composted. This is a great failing with most beginners and is difficult to determine, but if the physical condition appears good it is better to bed down the compost in a slightly under-composted condition rather than to delay. Over-composted manure will rapidly lose heat and the straw will have become so short that when spawned the compost will tend to become too compact, thereby cutting off oxygen required by the growing mycelium.

More important still, the pH value of manure that has been over-composted will be too low; that of under-composted manure too high. In other words, manure which has been over-composted will be too acid, and will become more so whilst the spawn is growing, soon reaching so high a level of acidity that the spawn will cease to grow. Though it may be rather too alkaline when spawned, the pH value of under-composted manure will fall slowly after it is spawned, and, provided the pH value is around 8·0, then a useful crop may be expected. It is thus better that the manure be slightly under- rather than over-composted.

As an example, once having a load of manure for which no room could be found in the mushroom house, it was thrown, completely fresh, but with a little gypsum added, into a shed which at one time had housed poultry. It was made up into a flat bed on the floor and was beaten down with the back of a spade and spawned as soon as the temperature had fallen to 70° F (21° C). Nearly 2 lb. per sq. ft. of the finest mushrooms

I ever grew were eventually gathered and sold for top prices. The experiment was never repeated, why I do not know, but it certainly confirmed the views of the old growers who made use of manure in a fresh condition. On the other hand, the same results may never again have been obtained.

Testing for pH value

Whether the compost is alkaline or acid is most important to the bearing of the crop, and this is where the pH test comes in. Tests should be made after the third turn so that it is possible to determine by scientific, as well as physical, methods when the compost will be in the correct condition for taking into the house. Fresh manure is alkaline, and is usually considered too much so to produce a heavy crop, though this was not confirmed by my small experiment. But perhaps the use of gypsum, which is slightly acid and has a pH value of 6·4, was able to neutralise the manure by the time the spawn came into bearing. Besides its physical properties in drying out wet manure and preventing greasiness, gypsum is able to neutralise the alkalinity of fresh manure so that it may be fully composted more quickly. Its introduction certainly revolutionised mushroom growing.

The pH value of the soil is an indication of the hydrogen ion concentration of the compost moisture, and the acidity or alkalinity varies according to this concentration. The pH scale extends from 0 to 14, with neutrality in the middle at 7·0, which is the pH value of pure water. A pH value of under 7·0 shows an acid reaction and when alkaline, the reaction will give a value greater than 7·0. A colour chart will denote the approximate values, the range of colours passing from deep purple, which denotes the greatest degree of acidity, to deep green, which signifies high alkalinity. One unit change in the pH value represents a hydrogen ion value of 10. For example,

90

if the compost shows a *p*H value of 5·0, it is ten times more acid than where showing a value of 6·0 and, as one extra turn is capable of changing the *p*H value by this amount, it is obvious that great care must be taken that the composting is not carried too far. It is also important that the correct physical condition coincides with the correct *p*H value.

Testing for *p*H is a simple matter, and a suitable method is by means of the B.D.H. soil indicator kit. This consists of a bottle of indicator solution, barium sulphate (a white powder), glass test tubes, and distilled water, together with a colour indicator chart, all housed in a compact wooden box to make for ease in handling, and so that the test tubes are protected from careless movement. The glass tubes stand upright, inserted through holes in a wooden support. The colour chart has a different *p*H value for each gradation of colour from blue through green and yellow, to pink and deep red. To test for the *p*H value, a sample of manure taken immediately after the third turn, is placed in a test tube, and a little barium sulphate added. The tube is then 3 parts filled with water and shaken up. A few drops of indicator are added, and the colour of the resultant solution is then compared with the colour chart and the *p*H value read off accordingly. If the manure arrives in a state of partial decomposition, a test should be made immediately, not waiting until after the third turn.

For the large commercial grower, the Cambridge *p*H meter is to be recommended. It is a pocket-size meter designed with the mushroom grower in mind, and can be carried in the pocket. It enables rapid testing to be done and with it, a *p*H measurement can be taken in 3 minutes. The meter incorporates a direct-reading indicator with a scale covering the whole *p*H range and utilises a simple circuit incorporating a miniature electrometer valve with the measuring and reference electrodes combined into a single unit.

A tiny plastic cup fits over the electrode unit to hold a small amount of the sample to be tested. The electrode system and two bottles, one containing a neutral solution of pH 7·0 for standardisation, and the other a saturated solution of KCl (potassium chloride) for replenishing the reference cell. Once connected to the electrode and switched on, the meter is standardised against the neutral solution which enters the plastic cup at the base of the electrode. The pointer is brought to pH 7·0 when readings can be taken.

The test should show a pH value of near 8·0, but not above that value. Should this be so, the manure should be allowed to remain for several more days in the heap, taking the test daily until it has fallen to a pH of this value.

If the manure is to undergo pasteurisation it should then be removed to the beds or boxes without delay, and after peak heating the pH value will have fallen rather more to a pH of around 7·6, which will denote that, subject to the physical condition being correct, all should be well.

If peak heating cannot be carried out, the compost should be taken indoors and allowed to heat up again. Then, as soon as the pH denotes a value of 7·6, which shows that the compost is slightly alkaline, it should be transferred to the tiers (or boxes) and spawned as soon as the temperature has fallen below 80° F (27° C).

As the spawn makes growth, the pH will continue to fall very slowly until it has fallen to a value of 6·2, which is the correct value for mushroom production. This denotes slight acidity of the compost. As the crop remains in bearing it will tend to become more acid. When the pH value has fallen to around 5·0, which will denote a condition 100 times (10×10) as acid as pH 7·0, the mushrooms cease to grow entirely, though the beds will appear to be full of spawn growth. It is, therefore, of the utmost importance to the commercial

Preparation of the compost

grower to ensure that pH tests are accurately carried out as soon as the physical condition of the compost would appear to make this necessary.

Fortunately, the physical condition of the compost denotes, with fair accuracy, the pH value, and some growers pay little heed to pH testing, relying almost entirely on their knowledge of what an ideal compost should be like. This, however, can only come after long experience, and the amateur should rely on science.

If the compost is black and greasy in appearance it will denote a high degree of alkalinity, and it will never grow a heavy crop, however much time and labour has been taken with its preparation. It is, therefore, better discarded, to be used on the land, and a fresh start made. Over-composted manure will tend to become too short and will also take on a lifeless black appearance, but here a pH test will denote excessive acidity so that by the time the crop has been a week or two in bearing, the compost will have become too acid to produce more mushrooms.

Sometimes there may be some difficulty in bringing what appears to be a satisfactory compost to the correct pH value. It may remain in the region of 8·5, and though another turn may bring down the pH, this may not be advisable for fear of the physical condition deteriorating. Where this is the case, the compost should be taken indoors and allowed to heat up again for about 48 hours, additional gypsum, which has an acid reaction, often reducing the pH to the required level.

Correct pH and physical condition should go hand in hand, and if all aspects of composting are given careful attention from the moment the manure is unloaded, not only will the manure be brought into a suitable condition in the quickest possible time but this will coincide with the fall in pH value.

A valuable new activator

Growers are now using a patented compost activator called Sporavite with up to 10 per cent increase in cropping. It is manufactured by Rumenco Ltd. of Burton-on-Trent, from fibrous molasses meal and EC. Feed, a by-product of the yeast fermentation of molasses. It provides additional carbohydrates from which mushrooms obtain their energy. These are present in Sporavite as sugar (20%) from the molasses which converts ammonia into bacterial protein when applied to the manure. It also supplies additional organic nitrogen (5%). Sporavite is added to the compost when the heap is stacked, or at the first turn, or half the quantity at each stage. It is recommended that it is used with small amounts of poultry manure at the rate of $\frac{1}{2}$ cwt. Sporavite and $\frac{1}{2}$ cwt. poultry manure per ton of horse manure. Where 50 per cent wheat straw is added to the manure, use $\frac{3}{4}$ cwt. Sporavite; and where straw is composted with poultry manure only, use 1 cwt. of Sporavite with 2 cwt. of poultry manure.

6—Making up the beds

Physical condition of the compost—modern composting methods—making up the beds—pasteurisation

Those who have had experience in mushroom growing will know, at a glance, exactly whenever a satisfactory compost has been prepared. It will have a satisfying mushroom aroma, one to excite the appetite, and will have an attractive appearance. It will not look 'green', denoting under-composted manure; neither will it be black, denoting over-composting and a greasy compost. Manure which is of light brown appearance will be lacking in moisture, but it will be better in this condition than where soggy, due to incorrect composting, or to possible exposure to heavy rains when nearing completion of composting. It must be remembered that manure will be much less able to absorb moisture the more advanced the composting has become, for which reason some growers make the final turn indoors or under cover outside.

When the compost is ready for the beds it should:

   (a) be rich brown in appearance
   (b) have no unpleasant smell
   (c) not be in any way sticky or greasy
   (d) have the straw neither too long nor too short
   (e) just leave the hand damp when a handful is squeezed.

Often, after the final turn, long thin-stemmed fungi appear about the heap. These are ink caps and will do no harm.

Liking similar conditions to the mushroom, they usually indicate that all is well.

Those who have visited a mushroom house where spawn is growing in correctly composted manure cannot fail to notice the sweet, rather pleasant smell, nor the awful sour aroma where the compost has been incorrectly prepared. Considerable experience will, however, be necessary before one can bring almost any heap of manure into just that right condition for the production of a heavy crop. I have known growers to 'hit the jackpot' the first time, who could never understand just what was all the talk about the art and mystery of mushroom growing. The art of growing good crops of mushrooms may be likened to making fifty runs against an experienced spin bowler on a sticky wicket. From the pavilion the experienced player can make it look easy!

Modern composting methods

There is yet another aspect to over-composting which has not yet been mentioned. This is loss of weight or bulk through excessive moisture evaporation, and the almost complete breaking down of the manure until it becomes too short. One ton of manure, with a little additional straw, will fill about 100 sq. ft. of bed area to a depth of about 7 in. Over-composting would reduce the area to about 75 sq. ft., an expensive business, considering the cost of manure and labour in its preparation.

In America it was Dr. Lambert who introduced a method of curing manure so as to increase its bulk. Assuming the same quantity of manure, 1 ton, water and gypsum are used in the normal way as the stack is made. After seven days the heap is turned as previously described and is allowed to heat up again for four days when it is again turned. After four more days the manure is taken into the house when the beds are filled and the temperature of the house is held at 140° F (60° C) for seven to eight days, during which time the beds will rise to a peak heat. The house temperature is then allowed to fall ten degrees each day until the manure temperature has fallen to 90° F (32° C), which will take five days. It is then spawned and the house temperature is held at around 65° F (18° C). It thus takes about 27 days from the time the manure arrives until it is spawned, the same as where, composting by ordinary methods, but with Lambert's method, the manure filled almost 150 sq. ft. of bed area and with no loss in weight per square foot of crop. It was thus possible to reduce the manure bill by almost half and there was also a great saving of labour in its preparation.

Dr. Sinden, also in America, went a step further, using similar methods but composting in less than half the time, and his ton of manure filled more than 200 sq. ft. of bed space to produce 400 lb. of mushrooms, double the normal yield per ton of manure. Sinden's method of rapid composting is now being successfully followed in this country.

In France, Sarazin has composted in only four days, using a rotating drum to mix the manure, but I have no knowledge of the amount of manure required to fill 100 sq. ft. nor of the crop yield. But these are experiments to be tried only by the experienced grower, and before they can be recommended, greater knowledge will be necessary.

That the time taken in composting and bringing the crop into bearing will greatly decrease in the next few years is a certainty, and it has been reported from America that stemless mushrooms have been grown in vats in an aerated nutrient fluid, the growing process requiring only 72 hours to bring the mushrooms to maturity. Eventually, we may be growing mushrooms in vats rather than in beds, and the whole concept of mushroom growing, as we now know it, will be out of date.

As soon as the compost is in peak condition and conforms to all known scientific and physical tests, the beds should be made up, whether they be shelf or tier beds, boxes or trays. Beds made up on the floor will not crop as freely in winter as in summer, for where there may be only a limited amount of heat in the growing-room, those beds which have a circulation of warm air beneath them will crop more freely than where placed on a cold concrete floor. Also, as warm air rises, these beds at the top of the house will crop more freely than those lower down. During summer the warmer weather will ensure sufficiently high temperatures for ground beds to crop freely.

Making up the beds

Where making the beds on the floor the area should first be marked out with chalk, allowing at least 2 ft. between the beds for paths. Flat beds will generally be made up indoors and the method is to shake out the compost over the whole area and to build up the bed until it is 9–10 in. in depth. This will be several inches deeper than where the bed is to be made on shelves or in boxes.

If the compost is in exactly the right condition it will be possible to tread it as the bed is being made. This will conserve both heat and moisture, but if the compost is slightly more moist than desirable, then the finished bed should be lightly beaten down with the back of a fork or with a spade. It should be said that compost to be used for ground beds should not be as moist as where used for shelves or for boxes, for here the circulation of warm air round the compost will cause it to dry out more quickly than when on the ground. For ground beds it is essential to ensure that the compost is not too moist. The hand should be only slightly moist when

Making up the beds

the compost is tightly squeezed, for when once the beds are made up, unless pasteurisation takes place, any excess moisture will be unable to evaporate as it will where used above ground. For this reason floor beds are always more difficult to crop well than shelf beds or boxes, and it must be emphasised here that *the compost for floor beds must not be too moist*.

Should the compost appear rather too wet for floor beds, additional gypsum should be sprinkled in as the compost is shaken out and the beds made up. There will be no fear that the use of too much gypsum will bring about an adverse chemical reaction. Use it as freely as necessary to dry out the compost, for spawn will not run well in wet manure.

It will be advisable to make the sides of the floor beds at an angle of about 45 degrees rather than vertical. This will enable the sides to be covered with soil, and will increase the area of mushroom production. Floor beds should not be made more than 6 ft. wide. Where side boards are not to be used, for surrounding shelf beds, the beds should also be made with sloping sides, which may be covered with casing materials, as well as the tops of the beds.

Beds to be made up in a greenhouse or rhubarb shed, or anywhere with an earth floor, may be made in a wooden frame, using 6–8 in. side boards, and these will be held in place by pegs which are driven into the ground on each side of the boards.

Where filling a house with tier beds, the top beds should be filled first, for the steam will rise to the top of the house; if the lower beds are filled first the filling of the top beds will be a most unpleasant experience. In any case, it takes a considerable effort to throw the compost up to the top tiers of a large mushroom house, and it can be exhausting work which is best done when one is fresh. Every effort, however, must be made to fill the house (or the room) in the same day, and this is especially necessary where pasteurisation is to be carried out. If all the tiers or boxes are not filled at one time, they will be at different temperatures when the time comes for spawning.

Where using side boards, make certain that the compost is pressed well down the sides so that it will not dry out too quickly, and so that there will not be any undulations caused by the sinking of the compost at a later date. As with floor beds, the compost should be thoroughly shaken out and then beaten down if not too wet. For boxes and shelves, a piece of wood about 15 in. in length and $\frac{1}{2}$ in. thick, and fitted with a handle, may be used for firming round the sides to ensure that the compost is made compact, so that all air spaces are excluded. As with floor beds, the amount of firming must depend upon the degree of moisture in the compost, but where tending to be on the dry side it should be pressed down as firmly as possible. There can be no hard and fast rule, however, for it all depends upon the state of the compost on the day the beds are made up. Where the straw appears to be reasonably long, the compost may be made more compressed than where it is short and possibly a little over-composted.

Experiments carried out at the Lea Valley Experimental Station under the direction of Mr. P. G. Allen have shown that the yield varies in proportion to the amount of compost used. After 6 weeks, the yield from 6 in. of compost was 30 oz. per sq. ft., whilst from 12 in. of compost the yield was 62 oz. After 11 weeks, the 6-in. depth of compost produced 42 oz., and the 12-in., 86 oz.—more than 5 lb. per square foot of bed space! But it is necessary for the compost to be of good quality to achieve these results. If not, deterioration will set in soon after the beds have given a first flush, so that there will be little advantage in providing any extra depth of com-

Making up the beds

post, for the crop will be too short lived for the spawn to make use of the additional plant food.

Wherever the beds are made it is important to ensure that the surface is left quite level and with no hollows, so that the casing soil will be of the same depth all over. The compost for boxes and shelf beds should not be made more than 8 in. deep, and where temperatures are adequate during winter 7 in. will be sufficient. But depths must be governed by numerous factors besides temperatures, one of which will be the duration of the crop. The longer the crop is to be left down the deeper should be the compost to ensure more prolonged cropping.

Two people will be required for filling the shelves, one to throw up the compost, whilst the other will make it firm in the beds, the work being taken in turns. Filling the house, unless it be floor beds, is not work for a woman but, for those growing only as a hobby, it is often possible to come to some arrangement with a local farmer or nurseryman for the use of two strong men or youths on the required day, and to pay extra in addition to their daily wage so that the amount may be shared with their employer and everyone will be happy. The operation will only take place two or three times a year in any case.

The day before the house (or room) is to be filled, the heat should be turned on. The amateur, filling his shed or cellar during summer, will need no heat, but where growing commercially, when everything should be done to ensure a successful crop, some heat is necessary to dry out the surface of the beds, for there will be condensation due to the steaming of the manure. Owing to the extreme humidity and the heat from the manure, a temperature of no more than 50° F (10° C) should be maintained as the house is being filled, whilst all doors and ventilators should be opened and the air-circulating fans brought into operation.

Pasteurisation

Then, as soon as the house is filled, all ventilators should be closed, leaving open only those necessary for the removal of carbon dioxide. The floors are swept clean and any pieces of straw trailing over the side boards should be pressed back to give the beds a tidy appearance. The doors should be tightly closed, or, where filling one room of a building, this should be sealed off from the rest. The temperature of the house is now raised to coincide with the natural rise in the temperature of the compost, depending upon the degree of insulation. Little artificial heat may be required. Pasteurisation is now commencing. This is the preparation of the compost taken to its final conclusion.

It is desirable that the temperature be raised to between 120° and 130° F (48° and 54° C), and this high temperature will be obtained only where there is reliable insulation. Two inches of fibre-glass insulation will make a difference of more than 20° F (10° C) between the outside and inside temperature of a mushroom house, so that 6 in. of insulation will be required to raise the house to approximately 120° F (52° C) where the outside temperature is approximately 60° F (16° C). Though the cost of providing such thickness of insulation will not be cheap, there will be a great saving of fuel during pasteurisation and throughout the winter cropping period.

It will take about three days to bring the house to the required temperature for pasteurisation, but as the top beds will attain a higher temperature than the lower beds, care must be taken to ensure that the heat at the top of the house does not exceed 135° F (57° C) or, to be on the safe side, 130° F (54° C), which is sufficiently high to pasteurise the compost. The temperature around the lower beds will be about 120° F (48° C) when it is 130° F (54° C) at the top of the house. The fans should be brought into action if there is any danger of the temperature exceeding 140° F (60° C), which would make the compost entirely unsuitable for mushroom cultivation.

The temperature of the house and of the beds will take four days to attain peak heat and, after holding this temperature for about 12 hours, any artificial heat should be reduced, so that the temperature will gradually fall. Just as the temperature will take about five days to reach its peak so it will take about five days to fall to 80° F (27° C). The beds should then be spawned at once.

During the whole of the pasteurisation period, temperatures both at the top and bottom of the house should be carefully recorded so that they do not exceed 140° F (60° C), and also so that the spawn may be inserted at the exact time. This should be under the care of an experienced person, for any carelessness will mean a reduction of crop. Air thermometers should hang in the house and hot-bed thermometers should be inserted in both top and bottom beds, though where there are only three tiers one inserted in the middle bed is all that is necessary. Readings should be taken twice daily to ensure that everything is going according to plan.

Remember that where pasteurisation is to be carried out, the manure should be taken into the house just before it may be said to be fully composted, with a *p*H value of about 8·2, for after peak heating this will have fallen to 7·5, at which value it should be spawned. If the manure is taken to peak heat with the *p*H value below 8·0, it may fall too low by the time it has sufficiently cooled for spawning.

Pasteurisation will sweeten the compost throughout the entire house, and any surplus moisture will be driven from the beds. Also, if a temperature of 135–140° F (57–60° C) is obtained, almost all mushroom diseases will be eliminated

103

from the compost, though this will have occurred previously with the heating of the manure in the stack. Few pests, too, will be able to survive these high temperatures.

Good crops can be expected without peak heating and, indeed, if this cannot be done correctly it is better omitted from the schedule. It should be said, however, that beds which have been given this treatment will give much heavier crops and will be less liable to attacks from pests and diseases. Nevertheless, it is essential to guard against over-composting, otherwise the manure will not heat up, neither will it produce a heavy crop. Under-composting is by far the lesser of two evils.

Where capital outlay permits and growing is on a large scale, it will be advantageous if one house is converted to a pasteurisation house. This is only possible where the mushrooms are grown in trays which are filled and taken to this specially heated house to be pasteurised and spawned, and possibly grown on until such time as the casing is applied. The trays are then moved to a cropping house where a temperature of no more than 60° F (16° C) is maintained. As many as four and even five crops a year may be obtained from these methods.

On a visit to Darmycel Ltd. (Darlingtons) in February 1981, Mr. Norman Barnard said that they grew their mushrooms to a ten-week cycle. Each lot of compost remains in the growing rooms for that length of time and produces five flushes of mushrooms, one during each of five weeks from the time the first pin heads appear. This is just less than 1 lb. of mushrooms from each flush. To obtain this, temperatures are kept constant all the year round. The compost is in the house for two weeks before it is cased and mushrooms appear within 21 days of the beds being cased. After cropping, allow two days for clearing the house and sterilisation.

7–Experimental composting

The shortage of horse manure—using poultry manure—composting with pig manure—sawdust composting—synthetic composting

The shortage of horse manure has forced upon mushroom growers the need to turn to other forms of manures and fertilisers for the making of the compost. These new forms of the growing medium may be divided into two groups:

(a) those composed of animal manure;

(b) those made up entirely from synthetic or artificial materials, using no animal manure at all.

Probably the greatest success has been obtained where combining both groups.

Since the mid-1930s, considerable attention has been given to synthetic composts in America, where shortage of horse manure was already becoming acute. By 'synthetic' is meant composts other than those prepared from horse manure, and in this category may be included the load of elephant manure I obtained on one occasion from a circus. It consisted of several tons of droppings, mixed with wheat straw saturated in urine. The manure was prepared in exactly the same way as described for horse manure and gave the finest crop of mushrooms I ever saw, nearly 3 lb. of huge white mushrooms per sq. ft. The mushrooms were almost stemless and each one weighed between 5 and 6 oz. They were sold direct to high-class florists for almost double the usual price and the demand far exceeded supply. Would that my mushroom farm was situated near to a zoo or circus!

There is much to be said for a synthetic compost made entirely without animal manure, for the ingredients may be controlled by weight, and it may then be possible to determine what weight of crop is to be expected with some degree of accuracy. Also, the materials to be used for a synthetic compost will be obtained with a considerable saving of transport costs, compared with horse manure which may now have to be brought from a distance of several hundred miles. Often horse manure cannot be obtained exactly when required, whereas a synthetic compost may be made up at any time. A further advantage is that the materials to be used will not deteriorate and will occupy little space where being stored, and another is that synthetic compost will be free from pests and diseases.

It is also possible to control the preparation of a synthetic compost so that there will be less variation than where preparing a compost from animal manure, since the exact requirements of the mushroom are known from its ash content, and an accurate analysis of horse manure can also be made. The result is that a compost can be made up precisely to the needs of the mushroom.

However, one of the greatest difficulties for those preparing a synthetic compost is to persuade the compost to heat up correctly, for if high temperatures are not obtained, bacterial activity cannot convert the materials present into the necessary foods required to produce a heavy crop in exactly the same way as when using animal manures. I have, myself, come up against this difficulty on several occasions when everything pointed to a correctly prepared compost, and for some reason it failed to heat up, until dry poultry manure was added to the heap. A very large percentage of the numerous letters that reach me each week from those who have made a start with synthetic composts are about this same subject. But let us first consider the value of animal manures other than horse manure.

Using poultry manure

An excellent compost can be made from poultry manure, which is considerably richer in nitrogen and phosphorus than horse manure, though it is not so rich in potash. Today, with the large numbers of indoor poultry houses, poultry droppings are an inexpensive and valuable source of fertiliser from which to make a compost capable of yielding a heavy crop of mushrooms. There are, now, intensive poultry establishments in most areas, and transport costs should therefore be reasonable. Also, as poultry manure is so highly concentrated, no more than 5 cwt. will be necessary to compost 1 ton of straw, and only half that quantity will be needed if a special mushroom activator is used with the composting.

It is, however, important that the poultry manure be collected and stored under cover, preferably from confined birds which do not bring in moisture on their feet. If the manure becomes sticky, it will make a sticky compost, neither will it heat up correctly ; the main value of composting with poultry manure is that it is capable of attaining high temperatures when correctly composted. It is thus able to turn what appears to be a lifeless compost, lacking body, into one which has extreme vigour. Poultry manure exposed to the weather will also have lost much of its manurial value.

To compost poultry manure, first make the straw thoroughly saturated, then spread out a layer 12 in. thick over the required area so that the completed stack will conform to the same measurements as described for horse

manure composting. Over the layer of straw a good sprinkling of dry poultry manure should be given; remember that it
cannot be handled properly if it is wet. Then provide another
12 in. layer of straw, more poultry manure, and so on until
the ton of straw and 5 cwt. of poultry droppings are used up,
the height of the completed stack being about 6 ft.

The stack will heat up rapidly and will be ready for its
first turn in about five days. Gypsum should be added at this
turn, mixing it in thoroughly as the heap is shaken out and so
that the poultry manure is mixed well in with the straw. Two,
or possibly three, more turns will be required before the heap
takes on that rich brown appearance and measures up to all
the other tests which denote a compost capable of growing a
heavy crop of mushrooms. If the poultry droppings have
been kept dry the compost will be more easily brought into a
suitable condition even than where horse manure is being
composted, and only three days should be allowed between
each turn.

I have made up a number of high-yielding composts composed of horse manure, decayed oak and beech leaves, together with some poultry manure. The method is to stack the
horse manure, to which is added a quantity of the leaves described (no other kinds should be used) and some gypsum, and
to make a separate stack of saturated straw and poultry
droppings, also as described, but in this case half the quantity
of poultry (or pig) manure is used. After the two heaps have
been allowed to heat up for a week they are turned into each
other, thoroughly mixed together, and are then allowed to
heat up again before composting is completed in the normal
way. Where horse manure is scarce, this is an excellent
method of 'bulking out' without the aid of synthetic products.
As the poultry manure is so rich in food value, heavier crops
may be expected.

Experimental composting

Composting with pig manure

Pig manure will also make a satisfactory compost, but again only if it is used before it becomes sticky. This is not as easy as it sounds, but when keeping pigs I found that if fresh wheat straw was used in their sleeping quarters and this was removed on alternate days, or every third day during dry weather, the manure would be just as friable as fresh horse manure and no difficulty was experienced in preparing the compost.

Delegates to the 4th International Mushroom Congress, held in Copenhagen in July 1959, were told by Dr. Rasmussen, Director of the Mushroom Research Station there, that after five years of experiments he could now produce as heavy crops with pig manure as with horse manure. After making detailed experiments immediately after the war I had already arrived at the same conclusions and have no hesitation in recommending mushroom growing as an additional source of income to the pig breeder.

It should, however, be said at once that pig manure must be obtained completely fresh and must be mixed with gypsum each day as it is stacked under cover. The heap should be built around a small tripod to encourage a free circulation of air as the stack is being formed. The more pigs kept, the quicker will the stack be formed and the fresher will be the manure when ready for the first turn. Pig manure in the popular term, that which is removed from a sty after several weeks and is thrown into a heap in the yard, will be quite useless for a mushroom compost.

It is important, when composting pig manure, to prevent any stickiness at any stage of the composting, which is none too easy since the heap may heat up by anaerobic fermentation. This is fermentation without oxygen, and will reduce the heap (or parts of it) to a sticky, black mass. The whole heap should, therefore, be kept as loose as possible to admit air, and this is best done by turning the manure over a wooden trestle made 8 ft. in length, and about 18 in. above the ground; the heap should be no more than 5 ft. high.

Any additional moisture for the straw, which will be saturated with urine, will not be necessary. For this reason the manure should be collected under cover, for an excess of moisture will reduce the heap to a sticky mass, as would happen if it was stored outdoors during damp weather. Once pig manure becomes sticky it is almost impossible to dry out, and it will also fail to heat up correctly. Dr. Rasmussen, in his experiments, discovered that pig manure requires only $1\frac{5}{8}$th the amount of water necessary for the proper composting of horse manure.

Pig manure will also compost quicker than horse manure, and may require no more than three turns before the physical condition and pH value determines that it will be ready for bedding. Over-composting must be guarded against or the manure will become sticky. One ton of composted pig manure will fill only about 70 sq. ft. of bed area and its yield will, however, be considerably increased if pasteurisation is carried out though, as with horse manure, this is best left alone unless conditions are ideal.

It can safely be said that if pig manure is used fresh and is turned under cover so that it is protected from rain, there will be none of that unpleasant smell usually expected from this manure. It will, in fact, be sweet and mushroomy, just like any other properly composted animal manure.

Sawdust composting

In a previous chapter I stated that sawdust should not be used for bedding horses if the manure was to be used for preparing a mushroom compost. However, some experiments carried

110

Experimental composting

out in America with sawdust and various additional ingredients have produced nearly ¾ lb. of mushrooms per sq. ft. and, as sawdust is so very inexpensive, this suggests that some value may be obtained from using sawdust when better knowledge of its composting is made available.

Poultry manure was used with the sawdust to generate heat, in addition to corncob meal, whilst soya-bean meal provided the nitrogen. Various mineral salts to provide potash and phosphorus were also used. Where hay was added to the heap another ¼ lb. per sq. ft. was obtained. The use of sawdust, however, is only in its infancy.

Synthetic composting

Years of experimenting with synthetic composts have resulted in highly satisfactory yields being enjoyed from several formulas, but no compost has yet been devised which may be fully relied upon to take the place of correctly composted animal manures. Indeed, I have no hesitation in saying that I have never yet made up a high-yielding compost without the use of at least some animal manure, whether from horses, pigs or poultry. It appears that the droppings from animals are necessary to give body to a synthetic compost, to persuade it to heat up to the required temperatures by providing the necessary bacterial action, and to provide trace elements not otherwise present.

One of the great causes of disappointment where preparing a synthetic compost is that it is difficult to persuade the heap to heat up, however much water has been applied to the straw, and it is surprising how the heap will respond to the addition of the smallest quantity of poultry manure used in a dry condition, which will provide the bacteria lacking in the chemicals. Or, of course, pig or horse droppings may also be used.

To prepare a synthetic compost, it is important to start with straw containing ample supplies of moisture. Half-measures will not do in this respect, for it is necessary to replace the amount of moisture in straw saturated with the urine of horses, which will have been absorbed by constant treading. Natural urine provides both nitrogen and moisture, both of which form the basis of a mushroom-growing medium, and these substances have to be replaced.

To persuade the straw, which should be wheat straw, to absorb the maximum amount of moisture, it is best to break it up, chopping it into 4-in. lengths. An ordinary farm kale cutter will do the job, and for those with easy access to a farm, quantities of chaff may also be obtained for the taking away, to be mixed in with the straw. Where only small quantities are required, sweepings from the floor of a barn or round a corn stack will provide the straw in a partially broken and moist condition.

Large quantities of straw are best stacked outdoors, where rain-water will do a more efficient job with the saturating than can usually be done with a hose. It is, therefore, necessary to begin to make the straw thoroughly moist in ample time before the actual composting is due to begin, and if the weather is dry, then frequent use of the hose must be made.

It may be said that 1 ton of dry straw will require almost 1,000 gallons of water to bring it into a saturated condition before composting can begin, and this will be sufficient to make 300 sq. ft. of bed space.

There are a number of activators suitable for the preparation of a mushroom compost, but they are highly complex preparations, containing all the ingredients necessary to give a heavy yield. An activator used for composting garden waste will be of little use. A reliable activator or manure

112

substitute is Adco 'M', prepared by the Adco Company of Chatteris, Cambs. Users of Adco 'M' and other synthetic preparations are eligible for a subsidy under the agricultural fertiliser scheme, provided that the spent mushroom compost is used on the grower's own land; when claiming the subsidy a declaration to this effect must be signed. The subsidy is paid for amounts of 4 cwt. and over, and is, therefore, applicable only to commercial users. It contains a high proportion of organic fertilisers to assist with the necessary bacterial activity. Alternatively, one may make up the activator to the formula of the Mushroom Research Association. About 5 cwt. of activator will be required to compost 1 ton of thoroughly saturated straw, which will work out to about the cost of 1 ton of horse manure. An equally satisfactory compost may be made from pig or poultry manure at less cost whilst, if some form of animal manure is used to assist in the composting, the amount of activator to be used may be reduced.

The M.R.A. No. 1 formula is as follows:

	lb.	oz.
Dried Blood	336	0
Superphosphate	14	0
Gypsum	35	0
Sulphate of potash	14	0
Carbonate of lime	50	0
Manganese sulphate		12
Iron sulphate		12
Copper sulphate		2½
Aluminium sulphate		2½
Zinc sulphate		1¼
Boric acid		1¼
Ammonium molybolate		1¼
Chromium sulphate		½

The basic ingredient is the organic fertilizer, dried blood, which is rich in nitrogen and which is a suitable alternative to using urine. An excellent compost may be prepared by using 1 cwt. of dried blood to every ton of wet straw, together with ½ cwt. dry poultry manure, 30 lb. gypsum and 7 lb. superphosphate. This is a simplified form of the M.R.A. No. 1 formula. Most of the 'trace' element minerals are provided in the poultry manure, which will also provide more bacterial activity than will the inorganic compounds. For this reason, with whatever activator is to be used, some form of animal manure should also be used in limited quantity.

The method is to build up the stack by first placing a 12-in. layer of wet straw covering the area required on the stacking site, over which is sprinkled a quantity of the activator and then to add a 6-in. layer of straw, over which is put a layer of poultry, pig manure or horse droppings. Sheep manure may also be used if it can be collected.

In Holland, the Customer Compost Enterprise at Ottersum supplies more than 650 growers or 65 per cent of the mushroom production of the Netherlands, and the 4-acre composting yard producing 1,000 tons of manure a week is always in full use. The horse manure is supplemented by the following additional sources of food during the composting period:

> Urea, at the rate of 7 lb. per ton
> Calcium carbonate at 55 lb. per ton
> Cotton seed meal at 22 lb. per ton
> Superphosphate of lime at 15 lb. per ton
> Gypsum at 55 lb. per ton

These supplements are usually added before the second turn, and their use has become standard practice which the grower preparing his own compost would do well to follow.

Experimental composting

Another layer of straw and a sprinkling of activator followed by more animal manure should be added until the whole of the straw, activator and manure have been used and the heap is at least 6 ft. high. It is then allowed to stand for a week whilst bacterial activity enables it to attain high temperatures. Should it fail to do so, turn the heap, adding more water but taking care not to wash away the activator, and giving additional animal manure. Poultry manure encourages the heap to attain higher temperatures than any other form of manure.

The heap should be given a second turn after it has attained the necessary high temperature, and should then be allowed to heat up for a further five or six days. If the straw is short there will be little difficulty in the turning, but the ingredients should be well mixed in at each turn.

The number of turns will be determined by length of straw to start with, and by the ability of the compost to heat up correctly, but on an average three turns should be given before the final turn, at which stage activator No. 2 is added. This should be given at the rate of 1 part to every 4 parts of No. 1 (parts by weight) and is composed of:

	lb.	oz.
Superphosphate	14	0
Gypsum	70	0
Potassium bromide		$\frac{1}{4}$
Potassium iodide		$\frac{1}{4}$

If animal droppings have been used the superphosphate is best omitted or greatly reduced in quantity. After another five days the compost should be ready for the beds, and where pasteurisation is possible this should be done.

The actual time for composting a synthetic compost is about a week longer than required for composting animal manures in the normal way. It is necessary to prevent the stack from drying out where preparing less than a ton of straw, whilst it is important to ensure that the heap attains sufficiently high temperatures to bring about correct curing, otherwise the compost will lack the necessary food value so essential for a heavy crop. Care must also be taken to see that over-composting does not take place, for it has been shown that an extra turn when not necessary has been known to reduce the crop from a synthetic compost by more than 50 per cent. All of which goes to show that it is more difficult to average 2 lb. per sq. ft. of bed with synthetic composts than with animal manures. The synthetic compost requires greater attention to detail, whilst there is less margin for error.

The compost will be ready to make up into beds and spawn when it answers the same scientific and physical tests as applied to animal compost, taking care not to over-compost, or the heat and *p*H value will fall rapidly. The compost will appear rather lighter in colour and drier when squeezed by hand than animal compost.

There is another aspect to the use of a certain amount of animal droppings in preparing a synthetic compost, and that is where animal droppings are present, the weight of the crop during the first weeks of picking will be considerably greater than where animal manure has not been used. This early weight of crop is extremely valuable to the commercial grower, for if the *p*H should fall rapidly to terminate the crop, the beds will already have produced a valuable crop. Also, the grower sees a quick return for his outlay, whilst it may also be possible to grow almost three crops a year in the same house, clearing the crop after possibly two or three heavy flushes.

An alternative to dried blood in the preparation of a synthetic compost is urea, a fertiliser which, unlike dried blood, is inorganic in form. It has for long been used by French growers but, being inorganic, is not able to cause bacterial action, though containing 46 per cent nitrogen, as compared with 12 per cent in dried blood. If used with animal droppings the necessary action will take place, whilst the urea will replace the nitrogen of the urine.

The method used by the French is to bed down 12 in. of wet straw, and to sprinkle urea over the top. Then over another 12 in. is placed animal manure in a suitable form and so on, treading the straw until a 6-ft. tall stack has been built. To compost 1 ton of straw in this way, use 14 lb. of urea, together with $\frac{1}{2}$ ton of horse droppings, or 5 cwt. of poultry manure. Twenty-eight pounds of gypsum should be added at the first turn in the normal way. If less animal manure is given then more urea should be used. The preparation of the compost should be exactly as previously described.

There are a number of alternatives, each method requiring additional trials before one can be dogmatic on any formula. H. M. Reed in Sussex has reported heavy crops, using chopped pea and bean haulm, rich in nitrogen, mixed with horse manure, whilst he had obtained extended cropping by making up his beds over a 4-in. layer of dry pea haulm, the spawn with extra food.

In America Dr. Sinden obtained valuable results from using corncob and wheat straw, to which was added bran and brewer's grain in equal quantities and at the rate of twice the weight of the corncob and straw. To each cwt. was added 30 lb. each of gypsum and calcium cyanide, and 15 lb. potassium chloride. Every seven to nine days the heap was turned and when ready, was subjected to pasteurisation for as long as it takes to bring the pH value below 8·0.

Dr. Sinden also had success using 5 lb. urea to compost 130 lb. ground wheat and 450 lb. wheat straw. There are many alternative formulas, but the beginner should proceed with caution, realising that in spite of all that has been done during the post-war years, it is easier still to make up a reliable compost from animal manure than with synthetic products.

8—Spawns and spawning

The old-type spawns—pure culture spawn—various spawn types and spawning methods—conditions for spawn growth

The advent of pure culture spawn, in which certain strains of mushrooms noted for their vigour can be propagated under scientifically controlled conditions, has meant as much to mushroom growers as the Seed Acts have meant to gardeners. The grower must now find some other excuse for the failure of his beds to bear a heavy crop. He can no longer blame the spawn, with but one provision, this being that it should be used in a reasonably fresh condition. Spawn which has been kept on the shelf of the sundries' shop for perhaps several years may have lost much of its vigour.

The history of mushroom spawn is extremely interesting, from the time when the old mill-track spawn was collected, until the advent of the modern spawns which, during recent years, have revolutionised mushroom growing.

Robinson mentions that the old spawn was to be found in half-decomposed manure, where horse droppings have collected over the years and have been kept dry, such as in mill-tracks under cover, and in the earthen floor of stables. This was known as 'virgin' spawn and was, in Robinson's own words: 'the best that could be obtained.' The chunks of dry compressed manure were lifted from the ground and inserted into the prepared hot-bed. Notice that Robinson makes particular mention of the necessity of keeping spawn dry, confirming my own observations that field mushrooms are always more plentiful following a dry summer, whilst spawn planted in a bed of manure which is too moist will generally decay and produce few mushrooms. It is also possible to kill growing spawn by watering the beds too heavily.

In Britain the old-type spawn was made in the form of hard, compressed bricks composed of horse droppings and cow dung, which were beaten into a mortar-like consistency before being formed into bricks. When partially dry, a small piece of field spawn was inserted into the centre and covered with moist manure. The bricks were then placed over a mild hot-bed so that warmth could circulate around them. In a few weeks the spawn would have permeated the entire bricks, which were then removed to a dry, dark place to dry out and where they remained until ready for use.

This type of brick spawn is still used, and I must say that one of the finest crop of mushrooms I ever grew was from this type of brick spawn brought over from Paris by my parents. For my present I asked for some French spawn, and they brought back several bricks. The quality of mushroom was superb, but the use of our own brick spawn as an experiment at a later date, produced no more than an odd mushroom or two of dirty brown appearance. Which is, of course, exactly what is to be expected from brick spawn, for it is most unreliable. It may have deteriorated with age or the spawn 'run' may not have been complete in the bricks. Weed and disease spores may so easily be introduced, whilst the strain of mushroom cannot be relied upon. French 'virgin' spawn was, however, greatly superior to our native brick spawn and was sold to professional growers in this country to the exclusion of other spawns until the advent of pure culture spawn. This was one of the most important steps in the reliable cultivation of mushrooms, for complete faith could then be placed in the spawn even though the preparation of a reliable compost could not be guaranteed until the late 1930s.

Pure culture spawn

Pure culture spawn may be obtained as 'white', 'cream' or 'brown', and new strains are being continually introduced to maintain the vigour of the cultivated mushroom. The brown variety is the natural mushroom and is still considered to be the most vigorous form. It is better able to tolerate adverse conditions than the white variety, and so is to be recommended to the beginner. It should also be used where growing conditions cannot be scientifically controlled. Especially is the brown variety most suitable for outdoor ridge beds and for floor beds.

A pure white mushroom first appeared on a bed of mushrooms in America, and was to lay the foundation of the mushroom industry throughout the world. Like white bread, the white mushroom was in much greater demand with the public, though in my own opinion it does not possess a flavour comparable to that of the brown variety. Again, as with white bread, the white mushroom has always been produced under artificial conditions and lacks both the stamina and freedom of cropping of the brown variety. The cream variety may be said to come somewhere between the two, both in its vigour and flavour, but its selling qualities are superior to those of the brown variety, though less so in comparison with the pure white mushroom.

Where growing conditions tend to be on the dry side, such as in greenhouses or sheds where humidity cannot be correctly controlled, then brown mushrooms should be grown, for as these conditions will tend to cause browning of the caps in any case, there would be little advantage in growing the less vigorous white variety.

The beginner should try all spawns of pure culture origin, for I am convinced that, as with tomatoes, different strains suit different environments in the same way as the saying, 'horses for courses' goes. To discover the spawns most suited to one's growing conditions, it will be necessary to plant several varieties and makes in the same compost and to grow them in the same building, for growing conditions are never exactly alike, neither is the compost. Floor beds will also provide quite different results from tier beds situated at the top of the house, where degrees of heat and humidity vary considerably from each other.

The manufacture of pure culture spawn is done under scientifically controlled conditions which demand as high a standard of hygiene as a hospital operating theatre. Equipment and media on which the spawn is 'run' are sterilised in autoclaves, whilst the filtration of air during the incubation period ensures complete freedom from contamination.

The most suitable strain to grow is arrived at by testing one against another under controlled growing conditions, the selected mushrooms then being removed to the laboratory. There, in a germ-free atmosphere, the spores are taken from the gills to be introduced into a special medium in test tubes, where the spores are to grow. Whilst growth is taking place the medium which is to be used for spawning the beds is prepared before being inoculated with the growing cultures.

Various spawn types and spawning methods
There are three types of spawn:
(a) that made from composted manure;
(b) that made from a vegetable medium which is generally tobacco stems;
(c) grain spawn, which was patented by Dr. Sinden as long

ago as 1932, but which has only become popular in this country since 1960 with the use of trays for growing.

Spawn made from (a), composted manure, is still the most popular. Simply, it is made by washing and shredding composted horse manure and, after packing into quart-size bottles, is sterilised and inoculated. The bottles are then plugged and placed in a growing-room where they are kept in a temperature of 70° F (21° C) to encourage the cultures to permeate the medium. As soon as fully impregnated, the bottles are removed to the inoculation-room again, where they are used to inoculate another series of bottles containing the growing medium. It is this second-generation spawn which is put on the market and, so as to maintain its vigour, a new strain is then obtained and grown on in the same way.

This manure spawn is obtainable in either the moist or dry form. Dry spawn will start into growth several days after coming into contact with moist compost and for the beginner it is preferable that this should be used. If the compost has been bedded down in a slightly moist condition dry spawn will take little harm, whereas wet spawn may possibly be killed by an excess of moisture. Dry spawn will also keep for a considerable time and so may be ordered well in advance, to be used when the temperature of the compost has fallen to 80° F (27° C).

Moist or undried spawn must be used without delay and so must be ordered for delivery to coincide with the approximate date of spawning. As this is difficult to determine in advance, especially for the beginner, and should there be any delay in the temperature of the compost falling, the spawn should be unwrapped and placed in a cool, dry room until required. The value of using moist spawn is that it will begin to run as soon as introduced to the compost and there will be a gain of several days in the appearance of the crop. Against this, if the compost is too wet it will be adversely affected. Those new to mushroom growing should play safe and plant dry spawn, obtained fresh from the maker so that its vigour may be relied upon.

Each carton of spawn (it is now sold in polythene bags) was at one time recommended for 50–60 sq. ft. of compost. Several factors, however, now make it desirable to reduce this area by almost half and to use three cartons for every 100 sq. ft. of bed space. A bed more thickly spawned will give a heavier yield during the first two flushes, for mushrooms appear in 'flushes' with a short rest period between each, rather than continuously. This will mean that there will be a much quicker return for one's outlay during the first weeks of the crop, whilst at this early stage the beds will be less liable to be troubled either by pests or diseases. Again, as the spawn grows, the pH value of the compost gradually falls until it will become too acid to support further mycelium growth. Therefore, the heavier the crop at the beginning the more likely will the ultimate yield be greater than where the mushrooms are borne over an extended period. In addition to this, it may be possible to obtain such a heavy yield during the first few weeks that the compost may be removed earlier than usual and three crops may be grown instead of two.

As the wholesale price of manure spawn is about £1 per bag, using an extra bag or carton for each 100 sq. ft. will cost only 2p more per sq. ft.

Rettew's discovery that spawn could be made to grow on a vegetable medium resulted in his patenting the use of tobacco stems in this respect, for they are rich in available nitrogen, a necessary food for growing spawn. In the immediate pre-war years an American firm marketed this type of spawn in Britain and it produced some excellent crops. The spawn is crumbled and a small amount is planted at the same distance apart as for manure spawn. It will get away to a good start if the compost is not too moist and will bear a heavy crop, but tobacco-stem spawn has never become as popular in Britain as either the manure or grain spawn. Dr. Sinden's grain spawn is made from crushed wheat, barley or rye grains which have been specially processed so as to make the maximum amount of food available to the growing spawn. The use of rye grain is now most popular, for the grains are light and narrow and, weight for weight, there are twice as many in a carton in comparison with wheat, yet there is more mycelium on wheat grains. Though more expensive, one carton of grain spawn will be sufficient to spawn double the area of manure spawn. It is readily handled and may be sown by pouring into drills 1 in. deep, or a spoonful may be inserted 8–9 in. apart in the normal way, planting rather deeper than usual if the compost appears dry at the surface.

Grain spawn has achieved a new popularity during recent years for spawning trays or boxes which are stacked in the house or pasteurisation-room. A length of wood of the same thickness of the box and $\frac{1}{2}$ in. deep is fastened to the top of the two longer sides of the boxes to permit the grain spawn being scattered over the surface of the compost by means of a shallow 'bat'. This is done without unstacking the boxes.

Another method is what is known as 'through' spawning, whereby the grains are scattered over the surface, the tops of the compost being ruffled up to absorb the grains, when the surface is then firmed down again. A heavier rate of spawning will ensure that there are at least a few grains covering the top of the entire bed, with the result that spawn growth is more rapid and the crop comes earlier into bearing. Heavy crops are produced early in the life of the compost and before disease can take a hold, but grain spawn tends to exhaust

125

itself quickly, whilst those mushrooms borne after the second or third flush tend to be thin and light. Better quality mushrooms are produced over a longer period from ordinary manure spawn, and if the manure has been correctly composted to be capable of giving a number of heavy flushes over a prolonged period, then manure spawn will give a better account of itself, but its use will depend chiefly upon how long the beds are to be left down.

Initial mycelium growth from grain spawn is more susceptible to alkaline conditions than manure spawn. It is, therefore, important that the pH should have fallen to below a value of 8·0 before spawning with grain spawn takes place. If the beds are to occupy the house for only a short time there will be little fear of the compost becoming too acid. For the beginner, dry manure spawn is the safest. It must also be remembered that grain spawn sent out in a moist condition cannot be dried and must be used almost at once.

Conditions for spawn growth
After the compost has been spawned, the temperature of the house should be maintained at around 70° F (21° C) or just above. Between 70° F and 75° F (21° and 24° C) spawn growth will be rapid and this is desirable for it is essential that the spawn will permeate the whole bed as quickly as possible, not only because the beds will come all the more quickly into bearing, but so that competing fungus diseases cannot get a hold to the exclusion of the spawn. Should the temperature fall below 50° F (10° C) growth will stop altogether and, as with all growing things, spawn does not stand still. Either it makes headway or it decays, and the latter will occur should growth be held up. Especially is it necessary to maintain a sufficiently high temperature for quick growth if the compost tends to be more moist than desirable.

Like the temperatures, humidity should be kept as near to 70 per cent as possible, for below this point the compost will tend to dry out. Where conditions are not controlled, some growers cover the beds with damp sacking or even with newspaper to prevent the top of the compost from drying out.

It is now commercial practice to exclude any intake of fresh air during spawn growth. Fans keep the air circulating over the beds but whereas it was at one time thought necessary to remove all traces of carbon dioxide, it is now realised that this is not in the best interests of spawn growth. Not until the beds are cased and the mushrooms appear 21 days later is the air intake increased to reduce the carbon dioxide content.

Should draughts cause the surface of the compost to become too dry, it may be made moist again with gentle overhead syringing, using a mist-like spray, and never at any time giving so much water that it will trickle down to the growing spawn, when it will most likely cause it to die back.

Attacks from insect pests, whose eggs hatch in the compost to produce grubs which will devour the spawn, must be prevented by dusting the beds with pyrethrum powder immediately after spawning and regularly each week until the beds are cased. A more effective control will be obtained by alternating with Agrocide 3 dust. These non-poisonous dusts are applied by means of a rotary blower or dust gun.

Every other day the compost should be inspected, either by lifting the side boards or by lifting a small area of the compost, and if all is well and a temperature of around 70° F (21° C) has been maintained the mycelium threads will be seen running out from the pieces of spawn into the surrounding compost and even about the boxes or side boards. Within 10–12 days quite a large area of the compost will have become permeated and these areas which the mycelium has reached will have turned a lighter brown colour.

9—Casing the beds

Why is casing necessary?—when to case—casing materials—peat and chalk—casing the beds—soil sterilisation

Exactly when to case—that is, cover the beds with soil—has for long been a controversial point amongst growers. That the beds must be covered with soil before the mycelium is to bear mushrooms is well known to all growers, but why the covering is necessary is difficult to understand. There is also a wide diversity of opinion as to exactly when the covering should be applied. A few mushrooms will appear on the surface of the bed without the aid of any casing, but having no support they will soon fall over, and the mycelium threads will be broken before the mushrooms have fully developed.

It would appear that, as the mycelium from the compost 'runs' into the casing, which is the name given to the thin layer of soil or other material used for covering the surface of the bed, it finds little nourishment there and comes into fruit in much the same way that plants grown for their seed are best grown, in soil which is lacking in nourishment. Such a soil will bring a plant more quickly into flower and fruit and it will do this in preference to building up excessive foliage.

Mushroom News, published quarterly by Messrs. W. Darlington and Sons Ltd., described (July 1959) the experiments of Mr. P. B. Flegg at the Glasshouse Crops Research Institute, at Littlehampton, on the use of casing soil. With the permission of the publishers I will quote from their report:

'He [Mr. Flegg] has found a relationship between the level of moisture stress in the casing soil and the production of mushrooms; a dry or saline layer can stop production altogether, whilst increased moisture (low moisture stress) results in more mushrooms being formed. Fruiting does not occur on uncased compost as the moisture stress is too high, due to the presence of large quantities of soluble salts. If this concentration can be reduced by frequent watering, fruiting can be stimulated. Small-scale trials gave 1 lb. per square foot off uncased compost compared with 1·65 lb. per square foot from compost cased (entirely) with peat and chalk.'

Generally speaking, the casing is necessary to support the mushrooms and to prevent the compost from drying out too quickly. For this reason the exact time for casing must be determined to some extent by conditions inside the mushroom house, and also the condition of the compost when spawned. If the beds are on the dry side, or should artificial heat be causing the beds to dry out too quickly, they should be cased without undue delay, though the surface of the beds may be kept moist by gentle overhead syringing.

Mushrooms are produced in flushes, and with each watering of the casing to bring on a new flush a cool layer is formed, which appears to shock the mycelium growing in the warm compost into fruiting.

When to case

Exactly when to case is always a matter of controversy and no two growers are ever agreed on the subject. Some cover the beds a few days after spawning, for they contend that in this way pests and diseases will be excluded from the compost, whilst moisture evaporation will be prevented. There is, however, a tendency for the mycelium to grow up into the casing as soon as the beds are covered and before the compost is full of mycelium. This will give early flushes of mushrooms, but the beds will usually cease bearing long before their time, and upon removal it will be noticed that much of the compost will be entirely without mycelium.

My own method is to create the necessary humidity so that the compost does not dry out (for I always bed it down on the dry side), and the spawn is then allowed to permeate throughout the compost before the casing is applied. It will take about two weeks in a temperature of around 70° F (21° C) and a humidity of 70 per cent before the mycelium has completely permeated the compost. It will then have turned a greyish-white colour, very similar in appearance to the cylinder of spawn which was broken up and inserted into the bed. The spawn threads will be almost cobweb-like, and should they appear thick and stringy it will denote a too moist compost and usually a poor spawn run. The appearance of whitish mould throughout the compost will usually signify a good crop.

It should not, however, be assumed that all that is now necessary to obtain a heavy crop will be to cover the beds with some soil. I well remember covering several beds, which appeared likely to bear well, with soil which was of a clay nature and which had been removed from a building site. The use of peat in casing soils was then unknown and after watering the soil on several occasions this, together with the warm conditions in the house and a lack of correct humidity, resulted in the soil panning on the surface in such a way as to seal off the compost below. The result was that after the first flush few other mushrooms appeared, and what should have been a satisfactory crop ended in failure through lack of oxygen reaching the growing spawn.

Casing the beds

On another occasion I had obtained a load of sterilised soil from a local nurseryman and, not using it all, the balance was placed under cover to be used at a later date. Not realising that the soil could become re-contaminated by standing several months before it was used, this is exactly what did happen and the heavy first flush was badly infected with the horrible *Mycogone perniciosa* disease. Which shows that nothing should be left to chance when growing mushrooms commercially. Nor even for home use, for ordinary garden soil will generally be full of weed seeds and diseases spores, which will come into life in the warmth of the mushroom house, and could completely ruin what would otherwise be a profitable crop. Now having provided the right environment so far and with the compost now full of mycelium, it will be advisable to give the casing just as much care as was taken in the preparation of the compost.

Casing materials

The casing plays a large part in determining the health and weight of the crop, and the use of peat in the soil just prior to the Second World War resulted in some remarkably improved yields. Dr. Bewley has described how, with the use of peat, he increased the yield of an experimental bed from 2·45 lb. per sq. ft. to 3·32 lb., and this was increased to 3·66 lb. when sand was also added.

At the same time, Pizer and Leaver, working at Wye College, Kent, carried out a series of valuable experiments which confirmed Dr. Bewley's discoveries. They divided casing soil into four classes. Class I was a silty soil in which clay-loam was present and which had a pH value of 6·4–7·3. It produced a continuous crop and yielded 3·50 lb. per square foot. Class II was composed of a mixture of sand and clay and produced 2·50 lb. per square foot. It had a pH value of

6·1–7·6. Class III was similar to Class II but of a finer texture and with a *p*H value of 5·7–7·6. This gave a yield of 1·50 lb. per square foot, whilst Class IV, which was a fine sandy loam with a *p*H similar to Class I, produced only ¾ lb. per square foot.

The tests were being carried a stage further when war put a stop to further experiments, but it was discovered that the top spit of soil removed from pastureland gave a heavier crop than soil taken from below. The topmost soil should, however, be rejected because it will contain too much foreign matter.

If found that a trial bed cased with soil from a particular pasture produced no diseased mushrooms, then those growing on only a small scale might find it possible to dispense with sterilisation. But the soil must be taken from pastureland, and it must be used without delay so that risk of contamination will be eliminated. The soil should be obtained when excess rainwater has drained from the ground, and it should be stacked on ground that has previously been sterilised, and where it may be kept away from old mushroom bed compost. Garden soil should not be used, so where growing on a small scale either obtain a quantity of sterilised soil from a local nurseryman, or obtain good quality loam from pastureland.

Soil containing a large proportion of sand will be unable to hold moisture which, instead, will percolate through to the compost, killing the mycelium at the surface. On the other hand, soil containing an excess of clay particles will tend to pan with continuous watering, with the results previously mentioned. The ideal is a good quality loam which is a mixture of sand, clay and organic matter, for such a soil will be able to retain the correct amount of moisture but will be sufficiently open to allow the beds to 'breathe'.

Casing the beds

Where the soil has a high clay content it should be used in as rough a condition as possible, and one of the finest beds of mushrooms I ever saw was a huge floor bed in a glasshouse, where clumps of brown mushrooms covered the beds like giant tortoises. Here the casing was in so rough a condition that half-bricks and stones gave the impression that the soil had come from a building site, and perhaps it had. The stones enabled oxygen to reach the growing spawn and allowed carbon dioxide to escape.

Quite the opposite to this, however, was the casing soil on the beds at the late Mr. Harnett's establishment in Hertfordshire, which was as smooth as a putting green; finer-textured soil it would be difficult to imagine, and the crops were always magnificent, the tier beds being covered with mushrooms of purest white. The soil used was of an excellent quality loam, which was rententive of moisture and yet which was sufficiently open to allow the necessary oxygen to reach the beds. For my own part I prefer to compromise, a good quality loam being used, and all but the largest stones being left in the soil.

There is no doubt but that casing soil which is of a light, sandy nature will produce a light, long-stemmed mushroom, and that a soil which tends to have a high clay content will bear heavy, short-stemmed mushrooms. Again, we have seen that Dr. Bewley and the experiments carried out at Wye College confirmed that the addition of peat to any soil resulted in heavier crops, and I certainly found this to be the case when I first used peat in the casing soil in 1939. However, where peat was liberally used in a bed which contained a larger than average amount of organic matter, the mycelium grew dense and coarse and resulted in a lighter crop. In other words, soil removed from the top spit yielded a ligher crop where peat was used, but the peat produced a greatly increased weight where used with soil taken from a lower depth and which was almost free of organic matter.

It is important that the soil has not previously come into contamination with old mushroom-bed compost, and to ensure that it contains nothing injurious to mushrooms it should be removed from pastureland, preferably where mushrooms are to be found and which will denote that the *p*H is suitable. Where good quality loam, free from disease, is to be obtained and which has proved itself under scientific conditions, the supply should be used to the exclusion of other soils.

The soil should be dug when the ground is reasonably dry, for wet soil is unworkable. It should be passed through a screen or riddle of 1-in. mesh so that small stones will be included. Any vegetable matter as well as worms and grubs should be removed by hand.

Some idea of the quantity of soil required will be understood when it is realised that to case 1,000 sq. ft. will require 3 tons, and a barrowful will weigh about 1 cwt. The soil should be stored under cover until required, for it must be placed on the beds in an almost dry condition.

To the soil should be mixed some peat of horticultural quality. This will be less acid than peat used for bedding and other purposes. This is important, for the casing soil should have a neutral reaction of *p*H 7·0. This peat, being almost sterile, should be mixed in after the soil has been sterilised, if, of course, sterilisation is to be carried out, and similarly any lime used to bring about a neutral reaction.

Where granulated peat is used in the casing, and it may be obtained quite inexpensively either in bales or sacks, it is important that it is made thoroughly moist before being added to the almost dry soil. The peat should be saturated, just as straw is made thoroughly moist before it is used for

Casing the beds

making up a synthetic compost. Surplus moisture should, however, drain off the peat before it is mixed into the soil.

It is difficult to give any definite ruling as to the quantity of peat to be added, for this will be determined by the amount of organic matter in the soil. Where the soil has the appearance of being devoid of organic matter, then about two bucketfuls of peat should be incorporated into a large barrowload of soil, mixing it thoroughly. After this has been done the soil should have a more spongy, friable feel and should just stick together when tightly pressed. The soil ball should fall apart when given a gentle knock.

After the peat has been added, testing for pH should be done, and if this shows a reaction above 7·5 then lime should be added until there is a neutral reaction.

Peat and chalk

Most commercial growers have now eliminated soil entirely for casing mushroom beds. This is because soil is heavy and bulky to handle and must (or should) be sterilised. There is also the need to bring the soil considerable distances with high transport costs, where growers are situated in a city and have no supplies on hand. The idea is to use high grade horticultural peat mixed with graded chalk which may be obtained from most lime quarries.

Whilst greatly reducing costs of handling soil and the danger of introducing disease where unsterilised soil may be used for casing, I feel that the peat and chalk mixture, which will give a neutral reaction, should be used only by experienced growers. The mycelium will run into the peat casing very quickly, with the result that more moisture than desirable is extracted from the peat. Because of this the mycelium may begin to thicken so that it forms a layer in the casing into which moisture given at the surface is unable to penetrate.

The top of the casing may, therefore, be quite damp whilst the lower layer remains dry, and there will be insufficient moisture to carry the mycelium to the fruiting or pin-head stage. For those who are inexperienced in mushroom growing it will be advisable to use the popular sterilised soil and peat mixture, though soil is so widely different in texture that one should conduct one's own experiments until results determine the right mixture to use. It is, however, important to treat the casing soil with the same respect as one does the compost, for the casing does play an almost equal part in the weight of the crop.

The great advantage of using peat and chalk in equal parts is that soil may be entirely eliminated from the mushroom farm. This is important in numerous ways, for not only will unsterilised soil introduce more disease than the compost which will have been heated to high temperatures, but the transporting of soil where none is available, and the sterilisation where considered necessary, will be most expensive. Again, both peat and chalk may be considered to be almost sterile whilst they are light to handle, it requiring no great strength to case the beds where using the mixture.

The mixture should consist of two parts peat to one part chalk. The chalk should be the size of a one-pence piece and is added when the peat has been made moist. It will neutralise any acidity of the peat, but is also used to provide bulk. Having little or no food value, it is used in place of lower spit soil, which will produce a heavier crop of mushrooms mixed with peat than will the top spit.

I feel that this casing mixture has so many advantages that when experience has been obtained in its use, ordinary soil will be entirely eliminated from the mushroom farm.

I have obtained slightly heavier crops from the use of vermiculite, which is extremely absorbent, in place of peat; also

136

Casing the beds

from poplar-bark fibre, whilst boiler ash and clinker mixed
into the soil have given good results where the soil was on
the heavy side. Soil which tends to be moister than desirable
may be dried by adding to it slightly moist peat, dry boiler ash
and gypsum. It is, however, important that the casing soil is
in just the right friable condition when ready to use.

Casing the beds
The casing mixture may be brought into the house in barrows,
which have been sterilised, and from which the soil is thrown
on to the beds with shovels which also have been sterilised.
Or it may be taken straight on to the beds in galvanised
buckets where it is placed at regular intervals. If friable and
slightly damp it may be spread over the compost, either with
the hands, wearing a pair of strong gloves for the operation,
or a length of boarding may be used. The soil should be
slightly more than 1 in. deep when spread out. Less than 1 in.
of soil may mean that when the beds are watered moisture
may percolate to the upper layer of the compost and kill the
mycelium, and also insufficient casing may cause the mushrooms to fall over. A too greater depth will delay the appearance of the crop, whilst it is not economical to use more
casing than necessary.

Experiments carried out at the Lea Valley Experimental
Station to discover the depth of casing that will produce
the heaviest crop, would seem to show that this should be
just under 2 in. The increase in yield between using 1 in.
and 2 in. of casing was (in 1963) as much as 1 lb. of mushrooms per sq. ft. of bed. Though the beds with 1 in. of casing
began cropping earlier, the eventual crop was less by 1 lb. per
sq. ft. than where the depth of casing had been increased to
almost 2 in. Perhaps somewhere between 1½ and 2 in. is the
ideal depth. Mr. T. E. Rucklidge, in charge of Messrs.

Darlington's Experimental Farm during the 1960s would case to a depth of $1\frac{1}{2}$ in., and he applied the casing after 12–14 days when the compost would be filled with mycelium. A mixture of Irish peat and chalk is used at the Farm. A decade later, casing remained the same.

With experience, it is quite a simple matter to gauge the necessary depth as the work progresses quite quickly, but the beginner should insert a stick or cane every so often to determine that the soil depth is correct.

Do not beat down the casing. In fact it should be left after spreading, with no more than a gentle pat with the board. If the peat and chalk mixture is used it should be left quite rough.

It should not be necessary to give water for several days. If casing has been done earlier than advisable, that is, before the mycelium has permeated the whole of the compost, it will continue to do so before beginning to run into the casing if it is kept dry. Nothing is gained by bringing on the crop before the mycelium has run through the whole of the compost. There will be early mushrooms but the crop will generally finish long before it should have done.

If casing is done after about two weeks, then another two weeks should elapse before the crop is brought on by giving gentle waterings, increasing the amount of moisture as the pin-head mushrooms appear.

It may be appropriate here to make mention of an interesting experiment described by Dr. Rasmussen at the 4th International Mushroom Congress. The experiment was what has now become known as 'shake-up spawning'. The idea is to shake up the compost two to three weeks after spawning whether growing in tiers, floor beds or in trays. After this has been done, the compost is made firm and level again when, in a few days, renewed vigorous spawn growth takes place.

Casing the beds

The bed becomes entirely impregnated with spawn and the pin-head mushrooms appear on time if the beds are cased about ten days after the shake-up.

This shaking up of the compost may be carried out as an alternative to heavier spawning, or it may be done in addition, to ensure that the mycelium reaches to all parts of the compost where it will obtain the maximum amount of nutrition. The results of Dr. Rasmussen's experiment have been striking indeed. From shake-up beds he obtained 6½ lb. of mushrooms per sq. ft. which, if it could be repeated by all growers and for every crop, would soon bring them into the millionaire class!

Soil sterilisation

All known pests and diseases peculiar to the mushroom will be killed at a temperature of 160° F (71° C). There are one or two exceptions to this, but of these resistant diseases we know little. It is my belief that more diseases are introduced with the casing soil than with the manure which, in any case, will have been raised to such high temperatures in its curing that all diseases will have been eliminated. For the commercial grower it is, therefore, important to play safe and to carry out some form of sterilisation with the soil. The amateur, too, would be best advised to use sterilised soil. This may take the form of sterilisation by chemical gases or by steam, whereby the temperature of the soil is raised to 160° F (71° C), at which point it is held for four hours. It is not necessary and is, in fact, inadvisable for the temperature to rise above 175° F (79° C) and, should the temperature exceed 212° F (100° C), the soil would be made completely sterile and so would be unsuited to supporting any form of plant growth.

A very efficient steam-sterilising machine is the Sterilatum. It is a metal container capable of holding 5, 10 or 24 cu. ft. of

139

soil, depending upon its size, beneath which is a fire chamber. The two larger sizes are mounted on wheels so that the machine may be taken from place to place. The serious grower would be well advised to invest in a Sterilatum, for they are easy to operate, will last a lifetime, and will ensure disease-free crops.

Steam is driven into the soil through small holes in the base of the container, a hot-bed thermometer being inserted at the top. As soon as the temperature registers 160° F (71° C) it should be so regulated that this temperature is held for about four hours, or for only about one hour if it attains 170° F (77° C). Higher temperatures should be prevented for they will render the soil more liable to re-infections.

After emptying the container, the soil should be allowed 48 hours to cool and recuperate. It is then mixed with the necessary peat and lime, and the *p*H value taken, more lime being added if required, so that a neutral reaction will be recorded.

The most troublesome of all mushroom diseases usually introduced in the soil is Bubbles or *Mycogone perniciosa*, which can ruin an entire crop where unsterilised soil has been used. Fortunately, this disease, together with most others, may be killed by treating the casing soil with formalin. It is one of the most effective of all sterilising agents and should be used at a strength of ½ pt. to 3 gal. of water; this will be sufficient to treat approximately ½ ton of soil.

The method is to water the damp soil with the formalin solution as the soil is formed into a heap. It is then covered with a tarpaulin sheet or with sacking to prevent the formaldehyde fumes from escaping, for it is these fumes (deadly to humans if inhaled) which will circulate through the entire heap to bring about effective sterilisation.

The heap should be untouched for a week, after which the

sacking is removed and the soil turned to allow the fumes to escape. The soil should be turned on alternate days for the next fortnight, when it will be ready to use. The soil should be kept under cover, and if treated with formalin about the time the compost is spawned it should be ready to use at the appropriate time.

Ground upon which the soil is to be stored and the manure composted should also be washed down with formalin solution both before and after the soil and compost have been prepared. Particularly is it important to sterilise ground which may not have a covering of concrete or asphalt. Preparing the compost on soil or grass may result in introducing Bubbles disease unless all suitable precautions are taken. Care must be taken, however, that the fumes do not come in contact with growing plants.

As an alternative to formalin, Sterilite soil disinfecting fluid may be used and will prove most effective. It should be used at a strength of 1 pt. to 10 gal. of water, the soil being treated as described. The soil should not be used for three weeks after treating and, as with formalin, care must be taken to ensure that the fumes do not come in contact with growing crops either in or outdoors. Treating the soil with formalin or Sterilite will dispense with the need to employ a steam-sterilising plant, though with certain soils steam sterilising is more satisfactory. The concentrated fluid is available in 1-gallon drums.

Wherever possible, however, growers should experiment with the peat and chalk method of casing, and so later dispense entirely with the use of soil and its tedious need for sterilisation.

10—Bringing on the crop

Care with watering—moisture and humidity—ventilation—
watering—trashing and filling in—termination of cropping—
re-casing the beds

Watering the beds to bring on the crop calls for great care for,
if too much water is given so that it percolates through the
casing to the compost below, the spawn will be killed should
it be in direct contact with the moisture. On the other hand,
if the casing is not kept uniformly moist throughout, and
there is a dry layer immediately above the compost, spawn
growth will be weak through lack of moisture. However, if
the casing is kept excessively damp and there is little moisture
evaporation, the spawn will grow coarse and stringy. In either
case there will be a reduction in the cropping of the beds.
Great care, then, must be exercised in providing the correct
amount of moisture, giving neither too much nor too little,
the amount being determined by the temperature and
humidity of the house.

Moisture and humidity

Where humidity is around 70–80 per cent and a temperature
of about 65° F (18° C) can be maintained, the beds will require watering possibly once every other day. The best
method is to give a light spraying with a hose which is fitted
with a fine sprinkler. A light sprinkling should be followed by

another to be given an hour later. If in doubt as to the depth to which the moisture will have penetrated in the casing, insert a finger, and if the casing immediately above the compost is still dry give the beds another light spraying. But do not over-water.

As the pin-head mushrooms make growth they will require additional moisture, and will shrivel up and die back if the casing is kept too dry. Likewise, the mushrooms will turn brown and die away before reaching maturity if the beds have been kept too moist.

If humidity inside the house is correct, then the beds will require only occasional watering, and if only a limited amount of heat is employed during winter, where the temperature inside the house may rise to no higher than 50° F (10° C), the beds should require watering only about once in eight days.

When spraying the beds it is important that every inch of the casing receives the same amount of moisture. Especially is it necessary to spray those parts of the beds close to a wall or side boards where the casing will tend to dry out more quickly than at the centre of the bed. Boxes or trays require great care in this respect for, having a free circulation of air on all sides, the casing will tend to dry out more quickly than with floor or tier beds.

As mentioned in the previous chapter, it is vital to have the casing a uniform depth throughout so that watering may be carefully regulated. Should the casing be too thin in parts, then water may percolate through to the compost, though the correct amount may be applied elsewhere. If too deep, the lower layer of casing may not receive sufficient moisture for satisfactory mycelium growth.

Quite apart from the humidity and temperature of the house, the amount of moisture required by the beds will be governed by the texture of the casing. Peat is able to absorb moisture much more readily than soil, and beds cased with a peat and chalk mixture will require watering less frequently than where soil is used. Here, again, soil of a heavy nature will be more retentive of moisture and will require less watering than a sandy soil. Peat mixed into the soil will reduce the need to water. This will be a saving of labour in addition to removing much of the risk of harming the beds through over-watering.

Where heating by electricity, or by hot-water pipes, it is important that the beds should not be too close to the heating or the compost and casing will dry out too rapidly. The beds should be at least 12 in. away.

As the pin-head mushrooms continue to grow, the amount of water should be increased, though never should an excess be given so that it will percolate through to the compost. The temperature of the house should now be lowered to around 56°–58° F (13°–14° C) to encourage the mushrooms to grow sturdy, whilst the growing crop should be given ample supplies of oxygen. This is essential, and whenever I have visited mushroom houses in which a sour, stuffy atmosphere prevailed, with the mushrooms turning brown before becoming fully developed, I had no hesitation in opening up all ventilators before doing anything else. The growing mushrooms require more oxygen than the growing mycelium, and as little as 5 per cent of carbon dioxide in the atmosphere will bring further growth to a halt, whilst half that concentration will cause the pin-head mushroom to die back.

Ventilation

It is important that fresh air is able to circulate over and around the tiers or boxes so that there will be no pockets of concentrated carbon dioxide. To ensure this, where there is a heavy concentration of bed area in a house or room, the circulating fans should be kept on whilst the beds are in bearing. During warm weather the fans will bring cool air into the house, and besides keeping the air fresh and sweet the temperature will be greatly reduced. As previously mentioned, giving the house a coating on the outside with bituminous aluminium paint will reduce inside temperatures by as much as 10° F (5° C) and it will be reduced still further by fixing ventilator fans to admit cool air. The Vent-Axia System, by which cool, fresh air is admitted by one or more fans, and stale air is removed by other fans, will keep the house cool and the atmosphere buoyant during the most oppressive weather. Excessive humidity whilst the beds are actually cropping will generally result in heavy concentrations of carbon dioxide, and must be avoided at all costs.

From experiments conducted, it has been shown that the carbon dioxide produced by the compost and casing soil of made up beds, which also contain mycelium, increases with rising temperatures. At 60° F (16° C) 5 units of carbon dioxide are produced per hour and at 70° F (21° C), 12 units.

Mader has shown that in addition, heavier gases are also produced, which lie immediately above the casing layer, and it is to keep this layer continually clear that efficient ventilation is necessary in addition to keeping the house clear of carbon dioxide.

The more mushrooms that are grown in a building or room, the greater will be the need to admit fresh air, for more carbon dioxide will be formed. Where the mushrooms are grown in boxes stacked to the ceiling, air-circulating fans will be a necessity, if a temperature in the region of 58°–60° F (15°–16° C) is maintained. In such a temperature 5 units of carbon dioxide will form every hour. Where a supply of electricity prevents the use of fans, and maximum cropping temperatures are maintained, then there should be an air ratio of at least 5–6 cu. ft. to each square foot of bed space. This is important where high temperatures are maintained.

Where beds are made up on the floor or where mushrooms are grown in a barn or some other place with an abundance of air space, concentrations of carbon dioxide will rarely be experienced, even at the height of summer.

The greater the humidity and the higher the temperature, the greater the chance of pests and diseases becoming troublesome, and apart from regular applications of insecticides between flushes, everything possible should be done to keep temperatures to below 60° F (16° C) during summer, and to maintain a regular circulation of fresh air about the beds. There should be no unpleasant smell upon entering a mushroom house, and over-wet beds and stagnant air must be avoided. The floor and bed boards may be damped down frequently during warm weather, and this will help to prevent too rapid evaporation of moisture in the casing. This will encourage humidity and more fresh air will be necessary. But there can be no rule of thumb as to the amount of moisture to be given, for it will depend upon conditions inside the house, prevailing weather, the form of heating used, and the nature of the casing. The beginner should tread carefully until he has learnt from experience exactly how and when to water the crop. More mushroom beds are ruined through careless watering than for any other reason.

Mushrooms generally appear in what are known as 'flushes', and in a temperature of 60° F (16° C) will take seven to eight days to mature from the first appearance of the pin-head mushrooms. In the same temperature there will be an interval of about eight to ten days between each flush. So that the white caps do not become pitted, sufficient moisture should have been given to the beds by the time the mushrooms are the size of a one-pence piece to carry the crop to maturity. For the same reason insecticides should be given only between flushes. The correct humidity of the house will, however, determine whether it will be necessary to give additional watering to bring on the growing mushrooms and, if the atmosphere is too dry, more frequent waterings will be necessary. This is why it is advisable to grow brown mushrooms where growing conditions cannot be scientifically controlled.

The results of the experiments carried out at the Lea Valley Experimental Station in 1962 show conclusively that the temperature of the house should be between 58° and 60° F (15° and 16° C). At this temperature, the crop from a 12-in. depth of manure after 12 weeks was 89 oz. of mushrooms, the same as where the temperature was kept at 66° F (19° C) whilst at 54° F (12° C) the final crop amounted to 79 oz. This was for winter cropping, and to raise the temperature of the house from 60° to 66° F (16° to 19° C) resulted in a considerable additional amount of fuel which was clearly not economical, whilst at the lower temperature the quality of mushroom was better and the incidence of disease much less.

Watering
Should it be necessary to have to water before a flush is removed, the house temperature should be raised to 65° F (18° C) for an hour or so, or additional ventilation should be given so that surplus moisture may evaporate from the caps without delay. Browning or pitting will occur only where moisture remains on the caps for some little time. Never water the beds just before the mushrooms are to be removed, or dirt from the hands will stick to the moist caps, thus greatly reducing their market value.

For the beginner to give the beds the correct amount of moisture is not an easy matter, for the beds will never recover from an excess of water, yet there should be sufficient moisture in the beds to carry each flush to maturity. Being composed of nearly 90 per cent water, mushrooms require considerable quantities of moisture whilst maturing.

After each flush has been gathered and the beds made bare, all roots and any decayed mushrooms should be removed, the holes filled up and the beds dusted with insecticide. The casing should then be made quite moist again, when the shock of cold water on to the warm casing will stimulate the beds into new growth and another flush will be commencing.

As the mushrooms will use up the moisture in the compost, rather more water will be required to bring on each successive flush.

The length of time between each flush and the duration of the crop will be governed by temperatures. During summer the flushes will appear in rapid succession, with only a few days between each, though cropping may be regulated by withholding moisture for several days after each flush has been removed. Reducing the temperature and admitting more air will also enable one to regulate the crop so that the mushrooms do not reach maturity at the weekend or during a holiday period.

My own method of watering is first to make damp any areas which appear dry on the surface, taking particular care to water around the edges of boxes or tier beds. Then, after about an hour, during which time other jobs may be done, the beds are given a light sprinkling over the whole surface. Again, in about an hour's time, a finger is pressed into the casing, and if the lower layer remains dry, the beds are given another light watering. This is repeated as soon as the surface again appears to be drying out. A too dry compost will bring

148

the crop to a premature conclusion yet, if the compost is too wet, the spawn will die back. All this demands experience and great attention to detail.

When watering, it is particularly important always to give a gentle spraying, for should soil be used for casing and a too forceful jet is used, this will eventually cause panning of the surface. This will cut off oxygen from the bed below, whilst it will be difficult for moisture to reach the lower layers of the casing.

The beds may be left undisturbed until the mushrooms grow weaker and each flush becomes lighter. This will signify that the beds are almost exhausted. This point may be reached after five or six flushes over a total period of about two months. It may, however, be more profitable to allow the beds to bear only three or four heavy flushes before the house is emptied and made ready for fresh beds. By obtaining a heavy initial spawn 'run' so that heavy flushes are to be obtained during the first weeks of the crops, the beds may have produced 3–4 lb. per sq. ft. within the first six weeks. They may be cleared after only two months' cropping to be replaced by fresh beds which, after a month in the pasteurising-house, will soon be ready to come into bearing.

Trashing and filling in
After each flush has been removed (and it will be better if the beds are entirely cleared within a period of 48 hours), the beds should be carefully gone over and all butts and roots removed. Begin at one end of the house and look over each box or tier bed in its turn so that neither stems nor roots are left to decay, possibly to cause an outbreak of disease. Often as many as a dozen mushrooms will grow from the same base, which may be more than an inch in diameter. This will leave a large hole where it is removed, together with its roots.

149

A sharp knife should be used for this purpose, the butt and its roots being removed in one operation. They should be placed in a trashing tray or basket, to be burnt as soon as the beds have been cleared. Do not allow any unwanted stems to remain, but on the other hand do not disturb the casing more than is necessary, for around the old root new pin-head mushrooms for the next flush, will already be forming.

The next operation will be to fill in the holes with a mixture of sterilised soil and lime, or peat and chalk may be used. If not quickly filled in, the mycelium round the holes will die back, for it will have no casing in which to make new growth. The holes should be filled in as soon as the beds have been trashed, the material to be used for filling in being made ready beforehand. Galvanised metal trays, which are easy to handle, should be used for the filling material, and a stainless steel trowel used to transfer the material to the beds. The surface of the beds should be kept quite level and, where the new casing has been applied, this should be made firm by giving a gentle pat with the back of the trowel.

When once the beds come into bearing they will require attention as regards trashing and filling in, and also as regards watering, treating for pests, and the gathering and sale of the crop, so that 1,000 sq. ft. of bed area will be a full-time job; the trashing, filling and watering being done during the day and after the crop has been marketed.

After clearing and filling in the beds, the paths of the house should be cleaned before the beds are watered to bring on another flush, raising the temperature of the house until the pin-head mushrooms appear. Mushrooms will soon start again from the holes which have been filled in with new casing material after a previous flush, though, as the crop is coming to its end, filling may be discontinued for the mycelium will not have sufficient vigour to grow into the new casing.

Termination of cropping

There are a number of reasons as to why the beds should finish cropping. We have seen that, as the spawn grows, it reduces the pH value of the compost, so that after four or five flushes the pH may have become as low as 5·0, which is a very acid reaction. Though the food value of the compost may not have been entirely utilised, the compost will have become too acid to support further spawn growth. For this reason, as many heavy flushes as possible should be obtained during the early life of the beds.

How to bring the pH of the compost to a more neutral reaction, has for long been the hope of growers, for there would appear to be no reason why the same beds should not continue bearing for at least 12 months or more. Neither watering with salt water nor with liquid manure will do much to prolong the crop, though where growing on a limited scale fertilisers may be used to add strength (weight) to the mushrooms of later flushes. Perhaps the growing mycelium forms a toxic substance in the compost which prevents the formation of more mushrooms.

In the 1930s, J. H. Harnett experimented by passing steam through the compost in an attempt to bring about a neutral reaction. The casing was removed and after steaming, the compost was re-spawned and re-cased, but only a very few more mushrooms were obtained. The compost appears to reach a point where it refuses to bear another mushroom, though the mycelium in both the compost and in the casing appears as vigorous as ever.

Commercial growers will remove the beds long before they have reached this point, for there is little to be gained by allowing them to remain in the house when they have ceased to be economical. There is little point in maintaining high temperatures when the mushrooms have become light and the flushes take longer and longer to appear. The beds should be cleared and the house made ready for another crop without delay.

Re-casing the beds
Sometimes, in spite of all precautions, an outbreak of disease may occur halfway through the cropping. If the beds do not respond to the treatment recommended it will be advisable to remove the casing entirely, and to re-case at once. This, however, will generally be necessary only where soil has been used in the casing, and where sterilised soil may have become re-contaminated. This may happen through over-long storage, and disease may have been introduced during the early stages of filling in. Should this be the case it will be advisable to re-case with a peat and chalk mixture. The spawn will re-enter the casing at once and a new flush will appear in about a fortnight.

11–Marketing the crop

Marketing the crop—picking—presentation—canning and quick-freezing—deep-freezing at home

The cultivation of the mushroom is only halfway towards the success of one's venture, for the marketing of the crop calls for just as much skill as in its growing. Where growing on a small scale, it will be quite an easy matter to dispose of the crop to one's neighbours, to friends and to local greengrocers. High-class delicatessen shops are always requiring quality mush-rooms, and are prepared to pay as much as 20p a pound more than greengrocers. Local butchers are also good custo-mers, for the snow-white mushrooms provide an attractive appearance when displayed in Sussex trug baskets lined with blue paper. Few people are able to refuse quality mushrooms when attractively presented, and the use of a trug basket gives them that 'country' look which is usually associated with mushrooms.

As soon as the first flush of pin-head mushrooms is ob-served, and there may be only limited numbers for disposal where the growing area is small, a visit should be made with-out delay to high-class food shops. When I first grew mush-rooms, several food shops, which later took more than 50 lb. each week, refused to buy just because they had never sold them before and they were not quite certain as to how they would fit in with cakes or savouries or with other choice foods. I was able to persuade only one or two shops to take 2 or 3 lb.

153

in small trug baskets in which they could be displayed more attractively, but I had to promise them sale or return. None, however, were ever returned and demand, which far exceeded their expectations, always greatly exceeded supply. But mushrooms were only beginning to achieve popularity in the early 1930s.

Marketing the crop

The commercial grower will need to contact a reliable wholesale merchant in each of the towns where it is thought that the mushrooms will make highest prices. Though transport costs must be considered, it may prove more profitable to send the mushrooms further afield in order to command better prices. For the same reason it is often more profitable to send the mushrooms to the prosperous towns of the industrial areas rather than to the London markets, which are often glutted with consignments from large Sussex growers.

But wherever the mushrooms are to be marketed, and those growing near to a large town will find an outlet for considerable quantities selling direct to hotels and supermarkets, stores and high-class shops, a visit should be made to a wholesaler of repute to find out exactly when he would like to receive consignments, the manner in which the mushrooms are to be graded and presented, and the most profitable market days.

Where sending a distance, it is usual to put them on rail in the early morning so that the mushrooms arrive before the market closes the same day. They will then be ready for sale in the early hours of the following morning. Where the mushrooms can be taken into market by road, they will always make better prices than where sent by rail if they are gathered early the same morning and are delivered to market around 7 a.m., before the buyers have left. They will catch the eye, if correctly presented, with their snowy whiteness.

The best marketing days are from Tuesday to Friday, there being little Saturday demand, but I always found that the Northern housewife was looking for a few mushrooms in the shops on Monday afternoon, after the morning's wash had been done and so that her husband's supper could be made more appetising where using up the Sunday joint. After the weekend there will generally be quite a number of mushrooms ready for gathering and, where situated near a town, direct deliveries may be made for Monday sales, also to hotels and cafés where flat, open mushrooms are favoured for serving on toast or for flavouring soups and meat dishes.

By making use of the telephone, most people are able to keep in constant touch with their customers so that, especially where local sales are made, fresh supplies may be taken in as soon as possible and whilst the demand is brisk. The use of a telephone will also enable the grower to phone his numerous retailers should the mushrooms make more growth than normally expected, due perhaps to a sudden rise in temperature. Hotels, restaurants and supermarkets can also contact the grower should brisk demand find mushrooms in short supply.

Picking
Gathering and packing the mushrooms calls for some skill. The mushrooms should be removed with clean hands, for dirty fingerprints will spoil the spotlessly white caps. The mushrooms should be quite dry before being removed, those growing singly being twisted from the bed whilst those growing in clusters or clumps from a single thick stem should be broken away from the base.

As the mushrooms will continue to grow after they are removed from the beds, it is important that wherever possible

155

they are removed just before the white membrane, or annulus, is broken. This is the part by which the cap is joined to the stem and which encloses the gills. When once this occurs, the mushroom will begin to deteriorate and will actually lose weight, whilst at the same time using up valuable food in the bed. The mushroom will have reached the peak of perfection as to appearance, weight and quality just before the cap opens to expose the gills. The best use may be made of the beds if they are removed at this stage. This is not, however, always possible and those just showing the pink gills will improve the appearance of the pack.

But it is in no way economical to allow the mushrooms to expand so that the caps have become quite flat. They will then have lost their attractive snowy-white appearance, whilst the gills will have turned dark brown and will be ready to shed their reproductive spores. If a mushroom in such an advanced condition is placed gills down on a sheet of plain paper and is not disturbed for an hour or so, the exact outline of the gills will be revealed by the fallen spores. If they should be packed in such a condition, and they often are, the spores will fall on to nearby caps, giving them a most unsightly appearance upon arrival at market, when they will command greatly re-duced prices. 'Flats', as they are called, are popular only with the catering trade and should be sold for this purpose.

To facilitate picking where there is no electricity available, a miner's headlamp should be used. Made of moulded plastic it is held in place on the head by an adjustable strap. The lamp, which is sold complete with two small batteries, can be moved to any angle whilst fixed to the head. A switch on the case operates the lamp. Besides its value in assisting in the picking of the mushrooms, the lamp may be used to give close inspection to spawn growth, or to detect a possible out-break of disease in the beds.

Marketing the crop

The mushrooms should be picked with one hand, taking care not to bruise the caps, whilst the base of the stem and any roots should be cut away with a sharp knife held in the other hand. The stems should fall into a box to be destroyed, together with any other stems and roots removed when the beds are trashed. The mushrooms should then be gently placed in a paper-lined basket, doing this before weighing, so that they are not handled twice. Where marketing in baskets holding 4 lb., which is the usual size, the basket should be lined with blue paper to display the white mushrooms to the best advantage. Any pieces of soil which may adhere to the caps should be dusted off with a brush or piece of cotton wool as the mushrooms are placed in the basket. Some growers, however, pick into trays so that any cleaning may be done afterwards. This, however, means double handling. If the weight of the basket is obtained before it is filled, this can be taken into consideration when the basket complete with mushrooms is weighed, and only one or two mushrooms may need to be removed to obtain the correct weight.

Presentation

Chip baskets or cardboard containers having the necessary ventilation holes are used. The mushroom should be placed in them stem upwards, and after the baskets are weighed the mushrooms should be protected by a cardboard cover on which is printed one's name and address. A trademark by which both the wholesaler and retailer may come to expect mushrooms of top quality should be used where marketing in considerable quantities.

For supermarkets and self-service stores, as well as for top-class fruiterers, mushrooms will find a ready sale made up in $\frac{1}{4}$-lb. and $\frac{1}{2}$-lb. punnets, covered with cellophane. The punnets which are manufactured by Arundel Plastics Ltd. of Beaconsfield, Bucks., cost about £20 per thousand for the size which holds half a pound of mushrooms. The mushrooms will present a more attractive appearance if packed before they have become too open. Mushrooms to be marketed in small punnets should be of such a size that about half a dozen should be obtained in every ¼-lb. punnet. This may mean that some will have to be gathered before fully maturing but, provided they are not removed in the 'button' stage there will be little loss of weight, whilst the later flushes will be as heavy as the first due to the quite small mushrooms not having exhausted supplies of food. They are placed in the punnets stalk upwards and a good portion of the stalk is usually removed when marketing in small punnets.

Waxed paper punnets or ordinary basket punnets may also be used, and are just as inexpensive. At least an extra 10p per lb. may be obtained for mushrooms presented in this way.

The punnets may be sent to market or shop on special fibre-board trays such as those manufactured by Bowater Fibre Containers. Each tray will hold 16 ½-lb. punnets and will add about another 2p to the cost of each ½ lb. of mushrooms. It must, however, be realised that, whenever there is a glut of mushrooms on the market, those most attractively presented will always command the best prices, and will also receive full co-operation from the wholesaler in their sale. The mushrooms should be so presented that both wholesaler and retailer may come to expect reliability, as a result of which they may be looked upon to perform their part in return.

This means that not only should one's mushrooms be suitably graded, but they should be quite free of any grubs, whose presence will be observed from the tell-tale holes at the base of the stem. Housewives who may discover grubs in the mushrooms may quite likely refuse to purchase more for some considerable time. As to questions of cleanliness, the grower of cultivated mushrooms produced under controlled conditions has an advantage over those who grow their crops outdoors, for almost all pests and diseases may be eliminated, and there should be no mushrooms marketed in an unclean condition.

In 1947, upon recommendation by the Mushroom Growers' Association, a body which has done so much to assist growers since the war, the Harding Committee evolved a scheme and made their proposals for the grading of mushrooms to replace the old National Mark packing. These were to be as follows:

Grade I. This should consist of button mushrooms of approximately 1 in. (about 3 cm) in diameter, and small cups which have the membrane completely intact. These mushrooms are suitable for high-class punnet sales.

Grade II. Here only selected cups should be used. That is, mushrooms which have their membrane at the point of opening or when it has just opened. Here the mushrooms will have reached maturity, the cups being $1\frac{1}{2}$–3 in. in diameter.

Grade III. Under this grading come the flats. These are mushrooms which are fully open, being flat instead of the desirable cup shape. Flat mushrooms will command lower prices and will prove difficult to sell during glut periods.

Where growing on a commercial scale, grading will undoubtedly prove advantageous, for packs which contain a percentage of flat mushrooms, possibly with long stalks, will not make such high prices as those from which such mushrooms are omitted.

The beds should be picked over as soon as the first mushrooms are on the point of opening their membranes, and care will be needed to consign them to market before they become too advanced to command top prices. In a temperature of 60° F (16° C) the mushrooms will grow from the stage where the membrane is breaking, to the flat stage in about 36 hours, so that no time should be lost in removing them the moment they have reached the peak of perfection. From then onwards the mushrooms will lose both weight and value. When once they have been removed from the beds they become highly perishable produce, and need to be marketed with the least possible delay.

It is not always possible, however, to market the crop when the mushrooms are in the peak of condition. This stage they may reach, in spite of all it is possible to do to retard them, during the weekend, and by Monday morning there will be a number which have to be graded as flats.

When picking, the best method of grading is to have three baskets which are held suspended against the side of the boxes or tiers by means of hooks. In this way the mushrooms are graded into each basket as the beds are cleared. Baskets capable of holding larger quantites than 4 lb. should not be used if they are to be transported a distance, for the mushrooms at the bottom of the basket will be bruised if there is too great a weight on top of them.

Again, where transporting a distance there will be some loss in weight, especially during summer. It is, therefore, advisable to add one or two small mushrooms to each basket to allow for this loss. Also, it will be difficult for the retailer to divide a 4-lb. basket into possibly 16 quarter pounds if there are not sufficient extra mushrooms to make up for fractions over-weight with each quarter. The retailer will make a mental note of the grower's generosity in this respect, and will ask for his mushrooms before those of any other grower.

To build up a good demand for one's product, it is important to have regular supplies available. There is nothing more disappointing to the retailer, who has built up a considerable local demand for one's mushrooms, only to find that during a long break between crops his customers have gone elsewhere. The same may be said for the wholesaler, for where buyers have to look elsewhere for quality mushrooms they will also make other purchases elsewhere. For this reason one should not change one's wholesaler for reasons other than perhaps disappointment with prices or for a similar good reason.

The question of length of stem frequently occurs between wholesaler and grower. Under the old National Mark packing, the lengths of stem for selected cups should not extend more than $\frac{1}{2}$ in. from butt to membrane. If the membrane is broken, then the stem length will be about 1 in., but it should never exceed that length. Too long a stem will detract from the appearance of the pack, and in any case the mushrooms should have been removed before the stems have become too long. Small, light-weight mushrooms with thin stems are not popular, generally making poor prices, whilst the beds will never bear the necessary weight per square foot in order for them to be profitable. This is why it is important to prepare the compost so that it will be capable of ensuring a good crop of heavy mushrooms. There may be some sale for stalks for flavouring purposes with hotels and cafés, but where there is no such demand it will be better to discard that part of the stem which is longer than 1 in. from the cap.

Always keep a detailed record of each crop, not only as a check against those packs sent to the wholesaler and for which payment may be made weekly or even monthly, but also for income tax purposes, and so that one may have the total weight of each crop from which to compare growing methods. Some growers record the weight of mushrooms gathered from each bed, but this is a tedious method, and where using boxes it is not practical.

Canning and quick-freezing

To move with the times the grower will need to consider the canning and quick-freezing of mushrooms. For the canned trade only very small buttons are required, which have almost no length of stem attached. Good prices will be required from the canners if the mushrooms are to be removed at this stage, but when it is realised that an 8-oz. tin of mushrooms retails for about 50p, it is to be expected that a good price may be obtained for rigidly graded buttons. They should be sent to the canner in a spotlessly clean condition, and transported with the minimum delay.

Flat mushrooms may be sold to soup and sauce makers who are prepared to buy on contract in quantities not less than 1 cwt., whilst they will also take supplies of button mushrooms for pickling.

With the ever-increasing demand for frozen foods, quick-frozen mushrooms would appear to have a large demand, and if cartons attractively packed were to be found alongside those of other frozen fruits and vegetables, the demand for mushrooms would be stimulated. Perhaps some interested commercial grower would find quick-freezing a paying proposition, but regular supplies would be required, whilst only the best buttons and small cups should be used. Quarter-pound packs would need to be made up and, as when buying fresh mushrooms in small quantities, the purchaser would prefer the pack to contain a liberal number of small, solid mushrooms rather than just one or two which are large and 'meaty'. It would appear that quick-frozen mushrooms would find a ready sale during the warmer months of the year when fresh mushrooms deteriorate rapidly both in weight and their appearance.

Marketing the crop

Deep-freezing at home

The home owner with a deep-freeze unit may take advantage of 'glut' periods, which mostly occur in July and August when mushrooms mature quickly and many people are on holiday. One can often obtain a 4-lb. basket of mushrooms for £1 or so and preserve them in the freezer for winter use. All types of mushroom can be used for freezing and there are two ways of doing so. Small buttons, cups and flats (which usually come at the end of a crop and are small and light) are placed in a saucepan with a little butter or margarine and seasoning. There is no need to peel them but if the stalks are long, reduce to 1 in. Simmer for just 2 minutes, remove from the pan and place in small waxed containers. Place in the freezer when they have cooled and put the unit on quick freeze for one hour. The mushrooms will keep for a year and will retain their full flavour. Use after thawing. Open freezing can also be done and this is especially useful for larger mushrooms (flats). Peel the caps and cut back the stems to about 1 in. Then place them, gills upwards, close together on trays in the freezer, or when quite frozen, place in containers and use when required.

12—Growing mushrooms outside

Labour requirements—selecting a site—making up the beds—care of the beds—growing in frames—other methods of growing outdoors—growing in grassland

Growing mushrooms outdoors is not to be recommended in preference to growing under controlled conditions. Not only is pest control during summer, a time when outdoor beds are most prolific in their cropping, most difficult, but at this time of the year on the mixed holding or nursery, labour is difficult to find for attending to the considerable amount of work demanded by outdoor beds. As beds in the open require covering with straw or bracken to protect them against rain, the material has to be removed and replaced whenever the mushrooms are gathered, and this means extra demands upon available labour. Also, when growing in outdoor beds it is not possible to subject the compost to peak heating, neither can the crop be controlled, as regards retarding or bringing on a flush, as is possible with indoor beds under scientific conditions.

The grower, however, might find that surplus land could be put to good use until it is required for the erection of additional mushroom houses, and where one is able to spare the time to attend to the beds good crops may be grown in the open, even if they are not as reliable as those grown indoors.

In William Robinson's *Mushroom Culture* appears an

164

illustration, dated November, 1869, of ridge beds in the open at Earl's Court. Robinson also describes beds from which mushrooms were gathered freely in July, 1868, from a market garden beside Gloucester Road Station, 'whereby using a coating of litter about a foot thick, over a layer of mats, it was possible to procure them in good condition throughout the hottest summer within memory.' The straw (or bracken) which is covered by mats, sacking, polythene or tarpaulin sheets, acts as insulation, thereby keeping the beds cool in summer and warm during the spring and autumn. If the tarpaulin sheets are sprayed with bituminous aluminium paint this will enable the beds to be kept as much as 10° F (5° C) cooler than the prevailing temperature during summer. For the cooler months, the sheets are reversed. Keeping the beds as cool as possible during summer will ensure sturdier mushrooms and will prevent the beds from drying out too quickly.

Where growing in the more favourable districts, it is possible to have outdoor beds in bearing from early May until almost the year end. It may be advisable to omit the month of August, when mushrooms are always in limited demand, and when pests are most troublesome.

Beds made up during the first days of April will continue to bear a crop until the end of July. If additional beds are again made up towards the end of July, they will come into bearing by mid-September, when mushrooms are always in demand. Given average weather conditions, the beds should continue cropping almost until Christmas, and they may be left down to bear intermittently until it is necessary to replace them in April.

It is not advisable to make up the beds before April 1st, for the cold winds of March will bring about a rapid fall in temperature of the compost and cropping will be delayed.

Nothing is to be gained by making up the beds too soon, exactly as with sowing seeds.

Selecting a site

The site selected for the beds must be thoroughly drained, for any excess moisture remaining about the base of the beds will soak into the compost and kill the growing spawn. For this reason it is better to make up the beds over a sandy subsoil, or over a thick layer of ashes which may be changed for each crop. This will prevent site contamination whereby the yield will become less and less. If the land is on a slight slope, so much the better.

Where moisture cannot escape too readily, it is advisable to take out trenches 6 ft. apart so that the beds may be made between the trenches to a width of 4 ft. at the base. Surplus moisture may then collect in the trenches, whilst there will be sufficient room to cover and attend to the beds. The trenches should be made about 15 in. deep and the same distance in width.

If the land is at all exposed, some shelter should be provided, either by means of an evergreen hedge or by wattle hurdles. Hessian canvas stretched across stout posts will also be suitable. Guard against having the beds beneath tall trees, where moisture would drip on to the beds and penetrate the coverings unless tarpaulin or polythene sheets are used. The beds should be made up near a reliable water supply, for considerable quantities will be required both for the preparation of the compost and for watering the beds during summer. Mice and moles, if present, should be cleared from the ground before any beds are made up, for they can do untold harm both to the beds and to the crop.

The compost is prepared as previously described but, as the beds should remain warm over as long a period as possible, take care not to over-compost. Neither should the compost be too moist, for a certain amount of treading will be necessary if it is to retain its maximum heat. An excessively wet compost will quickly become cold and soggy, and be quite unfit for strong and rapid mycelium growth.

Making up the beds

Ridge beds are used entirely for growing mushrooms outdoors. The beds are made 4 ft. wide at the base and approximately 3 ft. from base to apex. The beds should be rounded in shape, making it easier to case them whilst giving a larger cropping area. Ridge beds are often made up on the floor of an unheated house, also in caves and kilns. They do, however, require considerably more compost than flatbeds, though they make up for this by providing a greater cropping area in return.

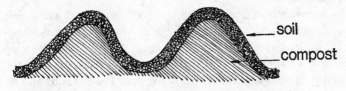

FIG. 5

Ridge beds. These are used entirely for growing mushrooms out of doors. The rounded shape makes casing easier and gives a larger cropping area.

To retain the maximum amount of heat, the beds should be made as compact as possible. First mark out the base of the bed to the required measurements, then put down a layer of compost to a depth of about 15 in., and tread over the whole area. After treading, the compost should still be quite springy. Then add another layer, again treading until the

167

bed has been made about 4 ft. high. The top and sides should be rounded off to make for easier casing.

As soon as the beds have been made up they should be covered with straw, so that the compost will not be harmed either by drying winds or by heavy rain. Covering will also prevent loss of heat. A hot-bed thermometer should be inserted and a reading of the temperature taken every few hours. If the compost is in a suitable condition, the temperature will quickly rise and will then begin to fall. Spawning should be carried out as soon as the temperature falls to 80° F (27° C).

The hardier brown variety of spawn should be used for outdoor beds; always use the less exacting manure spawn of pure culture origin. Plant the spawn over the whole surface of the bed, inserting the pieces 1 in. deep and 6 in. apart each way. This will give a vigorous spawn run, whilst the bed retains its heat.

Immediately after spawning, the bed is covered with straw or bracken which should be quite dry and should have been left under cover or in bales until ready to use. If the covering is wet, it will cause moisture to soak into the surface of the compost and may kill off the mycelium. The covering should be at least 12 in. deep; over it tarpaulin or polythene sheets are placed. They are held in position by tying to stout pegs inserted in the ground at the base of the bed. This will prevent the covering from being blown off during windy weather.

After about three weeks, provided the day temperature has been in the region of 60° F (16° C), the spawn should have made satisfactory growth, and the beds will be ready for casing. For this, it will be advisable to use a moist peat and limestone mixture, together with a small quantity of sterilised loam. This will enable the ridge beds to be cased more easily, for it is necessary that the casing should bind together, otherwise it will fall from the sloping sides.

The method is to first place a small quantity of the casing mixture around the base of the bed. This should be sufficient to cover the lower 6 in. of the bed to a depth of just over 1 in. It is made quite smooth and is held in position by firming with the back of a stainless-steel spade to which the casing will not adhere. Above this casing a similar quantity should again be given, a quick-spreading movement of the spade enabling the casing to remain in position. Or the casing may be thrown up by one person whilst another catches it with a board and spreads almost with the same movement. It sounds rather difficult but becomes quite easy with a little practice. Always start casing at the bottom of the ridge, and have the casing material slightly more moist than for flat beds, so that it will remain in position. It should also be free of lumps and stones.

Care of the beds
The straw covering should be replaced as soon as the casing has been completed, but from now onwards a small part of the covering should be removed almost daily to determine whether it will be necessary to water the beds. Never water unless the casing is showing signs of drying out and then give only sufficient to moisten the casing.

On mild, dry days the beds will benefit from having the covering removed for several hours, for if kept continually covered the beds will tend to sweat, so causing various moulds which may harm the crop.

The flushes are brought on in the usual way, giving rather more water when the pin-head mushrooms are observed, but withholding moisture as the mushrooms reach maturity. The covering must be removed with care as the crop becomes ready for gathering, for any rough handling will cause the mushroom caps to be damaged.

The beds are trashed and the holes filled in as previously described. As pests will become troublesome if neglected, the beds should be dusted with a reliable non-poisonous insecticide twice each week, generally when the straw is removed for the beds to be watered. A careful look out should also be made for slugs, which will quickly devour a whole flush if not kept in check.

Growing in frames
From the middle of May most garden frames will be cleared of half-hardy plants and often lie idle all summer. They may be made to grow a useful crop of mushrooms if filled with prepared compost to a depth of about 9 in. This should be made quite firm by treading, and three weeks after spawning the compost, it should be cased as described for flat beds.

To maintain warmth where the frames are being used for mushrooms during spring and autumn, and where the depth of the frame will allow it, straw may be used to cover the beds. This is not necessary during summer and only takes up more time in its removal and replacement when the beds are to be watered, or when the mushrooms are gathered. A thin covering of straw may be advisable where lights are used and there is condensation. Additional warmth may be given by heaping soil around the frame and, where bricks or cement blocks are used to make the frame, this will also prevent more heat from escaping than if timber is used for the construction.

Sunlight may be excluded by covering the lights or the frames with tarpaulin sheets or with lengths of hessian canvas. The direct rays of the sun would cause the beds to dry out too rapidly.

Ventilation may be given by raising the lights, and whilst

Growing mushrooms outside

the beds are being watered the lights are removed altogether. The beds will also benefit from being exposed to a few minutes of warm, gentle rain. To keep pests at a minimum the beds should be regularly dusted with an insecticide by slightly raising the lights and replacing with the least possible delay.

Other methods of growing outdoors

For those wishing to grow a crop of mushrooms at home, some success may be obtained, where the land is well drained, by taking out a trench about 2 ft. deep and 3 ft. wide. At the bottom is placed boiler ash or clinker to a depth of 6 in. to assist drainage and over this the prepared compost is placed and made firm by treading. An 18-in. depth of compost will tread down to about 12 in., which will allow for an inch of casing and about 5 in. of straw before the top of the trench is reached. Additional protection may be given by placing across the trench wooden planks, asbestos sheets or garden lights. The beds will require little moisture during a wet period, for sufficient will soak in from the surrounding ground. Being protected from cold winds, the compost will retain its heat for several weeks.

Heavy black PVC sheeting can be used to grow mushrooms outdoors. The sheeting is stretched over galvanised wire hoops to make a tunnel cloche. Make the bed just less than the width of the cloche and about 9 in. deep. The sheeting can easily be removed for picking.

William Robinson has described in his book a method by which large quantities of mushrooms were gathered when land for broccoli and savoys had been heavily manured and dug over. Spawn was then inserted in rows between the vegetable plants. He makes mention on a number of occasions, and not without good reason, that there would be mushrooms only if heavy rains were absent, and he noted that there were always more mushrooms beneath the maturing vegetable plants where the spawn was protected from excess moisture and sunlight.

Growing in grassland

There must be a considerable number of mushroom enthusiasts who wish to utilise their orchards, lawns and paddocks to produce some mushrooms, and why not? More mushrooms could be grown in the open than is so at present, for though one has little control on the yield, this being almost entirely in the hands of the weather, there is generally the chance of a good crop during late summer and autumn. Field, or naturally-grown mushrooms are more prolific following a dry summer, once again showing that they do not like too much wet. As an example I give the wonderfully dry summer of 1949 when during September and early October I gathered nearly 100 lb. of delicious white mushrooms over the fields of a single farm near Taunton in Somerset. Heavy dews followed almost 20 weeks without a drop of water, and mushrooms were in their element. Again, similar conditions in Eire during the summer of 1952 yielded a large crop of mushrooms during the autumn, and in England during the autumn of 1976, again following a particularly dry summer.

For those who wish to grow a surplus of mushrooms for home use, especially pickling and bottling for the winter and who wish to augment their income, a crop of mushrooms during autumn may be most useful. I say 'may' for, unlike those grown indoors or even in frames, outdoor beds or mushrooms in pasture cannot be controlled. The crop obtained chiefly depends upon the weather, though we can make certain contributions towards helping.

But first let us consider mushrooms grown in pasture in exactly the same way as the 'wild' mushrooms we love to find.

172

Growing mushrooms outside

As far as flavour is concerned, there are those who say, 'give us the field mushroom every time'. In a previous chapter I have detailed why I believe this opinion has become so general amongst lovers of mushrooms.

Any permanent grassland will be suitable, whether lawn, field or orchard grazed by poultry or any animals whatsoever. If the pasture is renowned for its mushroom crops, so much the better, for this will no doubt show that the acidity of the soil or certain minerals contained therein will be of correct proportions for a successful crop. To obtain a good spawn run, a quantity of compost should be prepared in the usual way during June. To plant up a field or lawn, carefully remove the turf to the width of a spade, lifting about a 2 in. depth. Then place in the open soil a forkful of the compost, pressing this down. The spawn must then be inserted at once in exactly the same way as described in the chapter on spawning. This being done, replace the turf and press down firmly by treading. A small quantity of the soil should first have been removed from the turf to balance the addition of the compost, and so leave the ground perfectly level once again. These applications of compost and spawn should be made at intervals of 6 ft. About the last week in June is the most suitable time for the planting.

During July and August the spawn will run to the surrounding ground, and if weather conditions are suitable during autumn, the result should be quite heavy pickings of mushrooms. It will be better to use the brown type of spawn, for this is better able to stand up to rougher outdoor conditions than the more highly cultivated white variety. Many growers apply common salt and superphosphate to the planted field during late July. This will certainly stimulate the spawn growth and will generally result in a heavier crop. Only a light dressing of superphosphate should be given, but salt may be applied in almost any quantity. Provided a sign is displayed stating that the mushrooms are cultivated and not growing naturally, the law is on the side of the grower and any trespasser can be prosecuted for entry on that particular field or orchard.

My opinion, for what it is worth, is that mushrooms so grown are the most delicious of all the various methods of cultivation, for they fall between natural and cultivated methods of growing mushrooms, or may be classed as resulting from a combination of both methods, and, whilst the quality is top grade, the flavour is equal to that of the natural crop, provided the mushrooms are allowed to mature to just past the button stage. They do not, of course, open overnight from pin-heads any more than will indoor-grown mushrooms growing in like temperatures. It is said that it may take as long as three weeks for a pin-head mushroom to reach complete maturity.

Those who possess neither orchard nor field, and who do not wish to mutilate their lawn, may like to try still another method of growing mushrooms, which proved a marked success a few years ago, when growing mushrooms in an orchard that had not been grassed down; an ordinary plot of soil would prove equally adaptable. This was first forked lightly over, taking in the usual prepared compost, then rolled flat. Over the top was spread a thin layer of dry poultry manure, and this again rolled in with an ordinary garden roller. Over this was spread mushroom spawn that had been crushed to a fine powder. Again this was rolled in, and watered. This was completed on July 1st, and after the spawn had been spread over the soil and rolled in, a large tarpaulin was placed over the ground. This was periodically removed and water applied when necessary.

The months of July and August proved warm, and by late

Growing mushrooms outside

August a fine crop of mushrooms appeared and remained in bearing until early October. To prevent the tarpaulin harming the mushrooms, a layer of straw was spread over the area and several large stones placed about it to allow the air to circulate freely. To those who may have a small garden border or plot of ground which is not used for producing food crops I give the above suggestion with some degree of confidence on a small scale, though I may have been just lucky!

13—Pest and disease control

'Mushroom-house sickness'—'cooking out'—fumigation—fungal diseases—aerosols

The warm compost, combined with high humidity and a temperature of around 60° F (16° C) inside the mushroom house, make an ideal breeding-ground for pests and diseases, and no crop is subject to so many as the mushroom. Indeed, the control of pests and diseases injurious to the mushroom causes the grower more worry than any other aspect of its cultivation, it being necessary to wage an incessant war against trouble.

When first growing mushrooms 50 years ago there were few effective preparations to use, and though much could be done to regulate humidity and temperature so as to reduce an attack from either pest or disease, little help was to be obtained either from fungicides or insecticides. It is also true that the less scientific the conditions, the more difficult it is to protect the crop.

'Mushroom-house sickness'

Probably the greatest cause of crop failure was due to 'mushroom-house sickness', a physiological condition with known cause, whereby the crops become lighter and lighter until they failed entirely to produce any mushrooms. The introduction of formalin in 1938, for washing down the house and its tiers, completely eliminated this 'sickness', and it was possible to grow a succession of crops in the same house with no loss of weight. The use of formalin, more than any other one factor, brought about the expansion of the mushroom industry in Britain in the years after the war.

Formalin is a colourless liquid with a strange sweet pungent smell, though it should not be inhaled. At a temperature above 60° F (16° C) the formalin releases formaldehyde gas. It should be used at a strength of 1 gal. of formalin to 4 gal. of water.

Having emptied the house, tiers which are made of wood should be singed with a blow-lamp, moving the flame slowly about the woodwork and directing it especially into the joints. This will do much to eliminate pests and diseases which may remain on or about the woodwork after the compost has been removed. Used compost should be taken as far away as possible from the area where fresh compost is being prepared, neither must it be dumped near to where there are beds in production nor where outside ridge beds are to be made up. It is, in fact, best put straight on to a lorry to be taken away and used on the land some distance away.

Whilst protein will have been removed from the compost, ash and organic nitrogenous substances will have increased. Thus, old mushroom-bed compost is extremely rich in its manurial value and, containing no weed seeds, it is valuable in using for potting, for making up a seed-sowing compost, and for lightening heavy land. When passed through a riddle it is also in great demand for golf courses as a 'green' fertiliser. One large grower I know has built up a profitable trade in sending out sacks of old compost in a dry condition to fulfil mail orders. Indeed, it is possible to obtain as much for the old compost as it originally cost. But in whatever way it is to be disposed of, the old compost must not be allowed to

177

contaminate the ground used for the preparation of fresh manure nor beds in cropping.

As soon as the beds appear to be coming towards their end they should be removed without delay, for the longer they remain in the house the more likely are they to contract disease. The tiers should then be treated with a blow-lamp, after which the house is washed down with a hose-pipe and all ventilators opened. The heat should still be kept on, unless it be midsummer, for spraying with formalin should now follow.

All ventilators must be tightly closed, the temperature raised to 60° F(16° C) and a tank of formalin solution made ready. This is taken into the house in buckets into which is placed the rubber part of the sprayer. Then beginning at the far end of the house, the walls, ceiling and tiers, as well as the floor, are drenched with the solution. The formaldehyde gas given off is poisonous so the work must be completed without delay. The entrance is then closed and sealed, and left so for 24 hours after which the ventilators are opened and the heating is discontinued.

A preparation known as ECA-55 is now being used to a greater extent than formalin, for it is a combined insecticide, fungicide and bactericide. For washing down a mushroom house it is used at a strength of 1 gal. to 25 gal. of water and is applied in the same way as the formalin. For it to be fully effective, a temperature of not less than 60° F (16° C) must be maintained for several days after treating, and before opening up the house.

Where trays (boxes) are being used, these should be placed in the house, after they have been emptied and washed, to be treated with formalin or ECA-55. The house and the trays should not be used for mushrooms for about 12 days, for this length of time will be necessary for the fumes to escape completely.

178

Pest and disease control

The ground for composting and for growing outdoor beds should also be sterilised between each composting, even though there may be a concrete floor. Nothing must be left to chance for, with all things, and with mushrooms in particular, prevention is always better than cure.

'Cooking out'

Even with the benefits to be derived from the use of formalin, it will pay the grower to guard against the building up of any particular trouble, either by giving his house an occasional rest, possibly during the summer months every third year, or by taking additional precautions. It is well known that where mushrooms are grown in greenhouses as a winter alternative crop to tomatoes, or as a summer alternative to chrysanthemums, diseases rarely become prevalent. Farmers and market gardeners have learned from bitter experience that it pays to rest the land occasionally, and the specialist mushroom grower could profit from their experience.

In addition to treating with formalin, the house should be given what is known as 'cooking out' treatment. Here the temperature is raised to 150° F (66° C), at which it is held for 24 hours. Eelworm is one of the most serious of all mushroom pests, besides being one of the most difficult to eradicate, but it will be completely eliminated where a temperature of 145° F (63° C) is held for 24 hours, which is another reason why it is so important to carry out pasteurisation of the new compost where a sufficiently high temperature can be provided.

High temperatures for 'cooking out' and for pasteurisation are readily obtainable by using the Baxi Hot Air Stove. A central fire box heats up air round the box which is released into the house by way of ducts, fumes from the fire escaping through a flue.

As an alternative, sterilisation by steam may be done, using a portable steam boiler. The steam is taken into the house by means of a rubber hose. The house should be tightly sealed for the steam to be effective.

Some growers carry out steam sterilisation or 'cooking out' before the used compost is removed from the house, and again after it has been removed and the house has been treated with formalin. The killing of any insect life and disease spores which might be present in the old compost will prevent infestation when it is moved elsewhere.

As an additional precaution, for it must be remembered that formalin is only a fungicide, a valuable idea recently passed on from America is to wash down the walls with wettable DDT, just before new beds are to be made up. This powerful insecticide remains active for several weeks and is especially useful in eliminating phorid and sciarid flies, which will be driven to the surface of the beds during pasteurisation, or when the compost heats up naturally after the beds are made up.

The insecticide Gammexane is also proving valuable in the control of mushroom flies. It should be used to spray into the compost just before it is given its last turn and when a high temperature at the centre of the heap will drive the pests to the surface. It should also be used at the time of pasteurisation, and again immediately before the beds are cased. Gammexane may also be used as an aerosol, the solidified form being fixed to an electric light bulb, when the warm bulb will release the Gammexane into the atmosphere.

The use of these efficient insecticides cannot be considered to be excessive in any way, for a severe attack of either the phorid or sciarid fly can play havoc with a mushroom crop. Where effective precautions have not been taken, whole flushes of mushrooms may be made unsaleable by attacks from the grubs of these flies, and when the house is treated with an insecticide in powder form, the flies may be seen to blacken the floor of the house with their bodies. One is advised to take every possible precaution at all times.

Where 'cooking out' and steam sterilisation are not practical, fumigation may be done before the old compost is removed, and again after it is removed. Washing down with formalin should also be done afterwards as a guard against 'mushroom-house sickness'.

Fumigation

Nicotine, sulphur and formalin are all useful as fumigants. They may also be used during peak heating. An agrocide smoke generator, containing Gammexane and DDT smokes, is also highly effective. To take each in turn: the nicotine, unlike the sulphur and formalin, will cause no harm to growing plants should any of the fumes escape. It is a powerful alkaloid insecticide best used in the form of Auto Shreds. This is very much like tobacco, and is placed about the mushroom house floor in small heaps. A No. 1 size packet is sufficient to fumigate 1,000 cu. ft. The shreds are lighted with a taper, and will smoulder sufficiently to fill the house with poisonous fumes. Nicotine fumigation should be carried out only when the mushroom house is being sterilised at the end of a crop or when the beds are at peak heat. Nicotine should not be used when the beds are cropping, and, if used as an aerosol up to cropping time, full protective clothing—including a respirator—should be worn.

Solidified sulphur is obtainable as sulphur 'candles', rather like night lights, the smoke being generated by lighting the wick. Sulphur is effective against insect pests and fungal diseases, but will leave behind deposits of sulphurous acid which tend to be harmful to the beds if used when the house has been filled.

181

The action of potassium permanganate crystals on formalin solution will release formaldehyde gas for fumigation. The method is to space small drums containing the formalin at regular intervals on the floor of the house, into the solution of which crystals of permanganate of potash are dropped. To fumigate 1,000 cu. ft., use 1 lb. of permanganate to 2 pt. of formalin, divided into four equal parts so that there will be a concentration of gas throughout the house. Like nicotine fumes, formaldehyde gas is extremely poisonous, and care should be taken in its use.

Agrocide and DDT smokes are both highly efficient insecticides, especially in the control of flies. The small generators are placed at intervals on the floor of the house; when a light is applied to the wick the gas is then given off from small holes at the top and around the sides of the generator.

Where using these fumigants, it is of the utmost importance to have the house completely sealed before lighting, leaving only the entrance open from which to make one's escape. This is then sealed up from outside. Great care should be taken to carry out the work as quickly as possible, for the gases are poisonous, though not so dangerous as the highly effective DNOC-sodium, and the phosphorus compounds, the toxic effects of which can be absorbed into the body by inhalation, and through the mouth and skin. DNOC-sodium is also highly inflammable. These preparations should be used only by those who have had special training in their handling.

The smoke generators should be lighted as quickly as possible, using a taper and working towards the entrance. As soon as one has left the house, seal up the door and fasten a sign on the outside prohibiting entrance for 48 hours.

Springtails and sciarid and phorid flies will be readily exterminated by using one of the recommended fumigants, whilst it has been established that nematodes will be killed

182

Pest and disease control

where the house can be heated to 145° F (63° C) for 48 hours. It may be said that nematodes will most likely have been destroyed during the heating up of the compost as it is prepared, but there is no guarantee that this is so, for the pests may remain on the outside of the heap.

Fungal diseases

Apart from insects, fungus diseases also find the warm, moist compost an ideal medium in which to cause trouble. Precautions should, therefore, be taken as for pests. Fortunately, most of the mushroom diseases can be killed if the compost is subjected to peak heating. Brown plaster mould is eliminated where the temperature has reached 126° F (53° C) for 12 hours, whilst the dreaded *Mycogone perniciosa* is unable to withstand a temperature of 122° F (50° C) for more than one hour. Fusarium, too, will be eliminated in half an hour at a temperature of 150° F (66° C), to which temperature the house should be raised during pasteurisation. Where using a mixture of peat and lime or sterilised soil for the casing, there will also be little or no risk of introducing these diseases.

Unfortunately both truffle disease and vert-de-gris will not be troubled by peak heating and so must be eliminated by other means. It has been found that 1 lb. of powdered copper sulphate mixed into each ton of compost when the first turn is given, will prevent the germination of both these diseases, whilst allowing vigorous spawn growth to take place. This preparation should, therefore, be used as a routine, for vert-de-gris, or mat disease in particular, can be most troublesome. A further spraying of the bed surface with dilute copper sulphate solution (the copper sulphate must be dissolved in an enamel bucket or glass jar) immediately after peak heating will be advisable. Where truffle and vert-de-gris have at some time been troublesome, it will be necessary to spray either the bed boards or trays with the solution immediately the house is emptied.

Zibimate, a selective fungicide, is also proving highly effective. This preparation was introduced by the du Pont Company of America, and it must be said that it is a preventative, not a cure. Its use has given excellent control of cobweb disease and of mycogone and verticillium, in addition to bacterial spot.

Zibimate should be used in the fresh condition, at the rate of 4 oz. per 1,000 sq. ft. of bed space. The first application should be given about a week after the beds are cased, and thereafter at seven-day intervals until the pin-head mushrooms appear. Afterwards, where disease may have been troublesome with a previous crop, it will be advisable to dust the beds between each flush. Some care should be taken in using Zibimate; so begin dusting at one end of the house, working towards the entrance. Then seal up for 24 hours.

Washing down the house with lime sulphur, Sterilite or formalin as previously described, will prevent 'mushroom-house sickness', and will eliminate all fungus diseases so that a new crop may be bedded down in conditions of complete cleanliness.

For sterilising the floor and soil in a greenhouse or rhubarb shed, which is to be used for growing mushrooms at some period of the year, Sterilite or Sterizal may be used at a strength of 1 qt. to every 25 gal. of water. Dig over the soil to a depth of 6 in. before applying the disinfecting fluid. Keep the house closed for two days, then drench the soil with clean water.

Sterizal or Jeyes' Fluid should also be used for disinfecting the boots of all who have entry to the mushroom house. A tray containing the diluted disinfectant should be placed outside the door to all houses so that those who enter are able to dip the soles of their shoes or boots into it. Tools should also be treated in a similar way.

Aerosols

The use of an efficient aerosol in the mushroom house is generally held to be the most efficient and economical method of insect control. The Mistosol 99 is reasonably priced and ideally suited to the small house. The machine weighs only 12 lb. and has a tank which holds 4 lb. of liquid, with a maximum output of 5 gal. per hour. The high speed $\frac{1}{8}$ h.p. motor develops 16,000 r.p.m., and the spinning disc system enables an excellent fog to be produced from the water based insecticides and disinfectants.

14—Pests and diseases

Pests: gall gnats—mushroom mite—nematodes—phorid flies—sciarid flies—slugs—springtails—woodlice. Diseases: bacterial pit—brown plaster mould—brown spot—bubbles disease—cobweb disease—damping off—La France disease—mummy disease — olive-green mould — truffle — vert-de-gris — white plaster mould—xylaria

Pests

GALL GNATS. This pest is also known as the Cecid Fly or *Mycophila fungicola*. At one time it was rarely a nuisance to mushroom beds, but it has now become as troublesome as the phorid and sciarid flies. It breeds even more rapidly, for the larvae also produce living larvae, which are very much smaller than the grubs of either the phorid or sciarid flies. Not only do they feed on the mycelium, but burrow up the outer edge of the stems from which they enter the gills of the mushroom, rather than the cap. The mushrooms will often turn a yellow-brown colour and will be quite useless. The pests can be exterminated in a similar manner to that described for other mushroom flies.

MUSHROOM MITE. As with most mushroom pests, the rate of breeding is so rapid that even where conditions are not particularly favourable, just a few will soon multiply to attain fantastic numbers.

Mites are not true insects, for they have a body consisting

186

Pests and diseases

of one complete segment only, and have four pairs of legs as against the normal three of an adult insect such as the fly. The species most troublesome to mushrooms is *Tyroglyphus dimidatus*, which is whitish in colour, and invisible to the naked eye. The mites feed on the mycelium, and on the decomposed straw, severing the spawn threads from the pinhead mushrooms, thereby causing them to die back. They also find the tissue of the mushrooms attractive, and will attack the caps of maturing mushrooms, causing irregular pitting which makes the mushrooms unsaleable (see Bacterial pit). A heavy infestation may also devour so much of the mycelium as to greatly reduce its cropping powers.

The mites lay their tiny white eggs in both the casing and in the compost, and also between the gills of the mushrooms. The eggs hatch within a few days, whilst the young mites will reach the adult stage within a week, when they, too, will lay more eggs. In this way a rapid build up takes place. Unfortunately, the pests are difficult to kill for, unlike most pests, they will be unharmed in a temperature of 150° F (60° C). Nicotine fumes will cause them no harm, and though some degree of control may be given by sulphur fumigation, this should not be done whilst the beds are in actual bearing.

It was the opinion of the late Mr. Harnett that the mites are usually introduced with the straw, so that some measure of control should be attempted during the early stages of composting. Gammexane, containing BHC, has given the best control to date, and should be dusted into the compost, at the rate of 2 lb. per ton, at the first turn. It is, however, best not used on growing mushrooms. This material is present in Lindane dust and in Agrocide smokes, which may also be used during peak heating.

NEMATODES. A powerful magnifying glass is required to see the wriggling bodies of the eelworms, which feed on the

187

mycelium, quickly turning what was once a highly satisfactory compost into a black, lifeless mass in which spawn growth will have completely vanished. The beds will, of course, produce no mushrooms.

Eelworms will be killed in a temperature of 145° F (63° C), maintained for 48 hours, so that they will usually cause little trouble where pasteurisation is carried out. Unfortunately, not all growers can subject their compost to such temperatures, and if they cannot, it is especially essential to compost correctly, to ensure that the heap attains a sufficiently high temperature for the pests to be killed. Compost which does not heat up correctly, and which is cold and greasy when bedded down, will be sure to invite trouble, for in such a compost eelworms will multiply rapidly, the almost transparent creatures giving birth to young as well as laying eggs. And when once there is a heavy infestation the worst may be expected, for there is no known cure.

Dr. Thomas, of Pennsylvania State College, found that nematodes were present in every sample of soil and manure that he investigated, but that they did not cause trouble unless present in large numbers. Where the compost is unduly wet and is proving difficult to dry out, there will be a greater chance of eelworm taking a hold. Manure which has been kept for a long period, exposed to heavy rain, will have become saturated and soggy, and will be an ideal breeding-ground for nematodes.

Unsterilised casing soil will also be a source of trouble, and it is a fact that soil which has been sterilised with formalin will be even more liable to contamination by nematodes, for formalin will have destroyed the parasite which feeds on them. Nematodes are even present in peat, where they thrive on its high moisture content.

Composting on concrete and storing the peat or steam-sterilised soil to be used for casing where there is a concrete floor will do much to prevent infestation. Keeping the compost and the casing material on the dry side will also reduce the risk of eelworm attack, for the pest will only breed and travel where there is sufficient moisture. Remember that an excess of moisture will not only harm the growing spawn, but will also encourage nematodes.

PHORID FLIES. When we talk of 'mushroom flies', it is the phorid and sciarid flies that are meant, and though the latter cause the most damage to the growing mushrooms, it is the grubs of the phorid fly which inhabit the compost, feeding on the growing spawn. A heavy infestation has been known to kill the entire mycelium, and the compost has had to be removed, being no longer capable of producing a crop.

The phorid fly, *Megaselia halterata*, which is also known as the Manure Fly, has a thicker body than the sciarid, whilst its larvae are about two-thirds the length of those of the sciarid. The phorid lays its eggs in the compost and in six days they hatch out into shiny, yellow grubs, which immediately start to devour the mycelium. After ten days they pupate and emerge as flies to lay their eggs and commence the cycle once again. It is, therefore, important to dust the beds as a matter of routine. This should be done every ten to fourteen days from the time of spawning, for it is easier to kill the pest in the fly stage rather than the larval one.

The great trouble with which the grower has to contend in dealing with mushroom flies is that, as the crop requires fresh air, the flies will enter through the ventilators throughout the life of the crop, and so it is never safe to assume that the flies have been completely exterminated at any time. Fumigating or dusting must, therefore, be continued throughout the life of the crop.

Nicotine fumigating in the form of Auto Shreds may be

done until the appearance of the pin-head mushrooms, and between flushes when the beds have been cleared, but it is toxic and must not be used on growing mushrooms.

The most satisfactory method of routine treatment of the beds against fly is to seal up the house for several hours and, using an efficient dusting machine or bellows, to dust the beds with pyrethrum powder, or with BHC (between flushes). The powder will remain suspended in the atmosphere for several hours and will kill any flies. There will, however, be grubs still in the compost doing their damage, and another dusting should be carried out in about 12 days, after they pupate. So that there will be no ill effects, dusting should be done only between flushes.

SCIARID FLIES. These are the most destructive of all mushroom pests, doing damage to growing mushrooms that must amount to thousands of pounds annually. *Sciara coprophila* lays its eggs in both the compost and casing. The grubs hatch out in six days and, as a single female is capable of laying more than 300 eggs, it will be realised just what damage the grubs can do. The grubs are longer than those of the phorid fly, and have a black head. They feed on the compost itself and on the mycelium, but they cause most damage by tunnelling up into the stem and cap of the growing mushroom, where they remain when the mushroom is gathered, to make it quite unsaleable. Whole flushes may be completely ruined by the grubs, which become fully grown in 14 days, and pupate in another six days in a temperature of around 65° F (18° C).

Trouble from the pest will, of course, be kept down where temperature does not exceed 55° F (13° C), but something more effective is needed if the crop is to be safeguarded. Fumigating or dusting the beds, as described for the phorid fly, will be effective if carried out as routine between flushes. Commercial growers add to the casing 10 oz. of Dimilin per

Pests and diseases

1,000 sq. ft. of bed area. Dimilin is a wettable powder which acts as a stomach poison on the sciarid.

SLUGS. On floor beds, and where growing mushrooms outdoors, slugs may cause considerable damage during a damp season by devouring whole mushrooms overnight. Regular inspection of the beds by torchlight will enable any slugs to be removed by hand and where growing outdoors the pests may be kept away by watering the ground around the beds with liquid Slugit.

SPRINGTAILS. This is a pest which often proves troublesome where growing mushrooms in glasshouses, and especially where peak heating is not possible. Where a temperature of 140° F (60° C) can be given and maintained for 12 hours, all springtails will be killed; thus large numbers will die if the compost is correctly prepared and attains the high temperatures possible where there is correct bacterial activity. It is therefore most important, where peak heating is impossible, to compost correctly.

The springtail, *Achorutes armatus*, is about $\frac{1}{16}$ in. in length, and is of a silvery-blue colour. Using its tail as a lever, the pest springs or hops several inches at a time. It may prove troublesome where mushrooms are grown in barns and old buildings, where it hides in the cracks of the walls or about the rafters. For this reason it will be advisable to render the walls with cement on the inside.

The pests enter the compost where they lay their eggs and these hatch out in a few days, to devour the mycelium in the same way as do mites. They are, however, more easily controlled, for besides being killed by high temperatures they will be eliminated by fumigating with nicotine in the form of Auto Shreds. They may also be kept to a minimum by the addition of 2 lb. of BHC dust to every ton of compost, added at the first turn.

Where peak heating can be done, fumigating with Agrocide smoke at this time will provide an additional check to the
pest. Nothing should be left to chance, for should an attack
take on serious proportions the pests will swarm on to the
growing mushrooms, devouring the stems from the inside
and causing the mushrooms to collapse.

WOODLICE. These pests may enter the beds from the walls
and woodwork of old buildings, or they may be carried inside
with the compost if it has not been correctly cured. They are
unable to survive a temperature of 140° F (60° C) for several
hours, and so most of them will be eliminated either during
composting or at peak heating. Others which may enter the
beds during cropping will feed on the mycelium and the
growing mushrooms, and where present in quantity will
cause considerable damage. Fortunately the pest is readily
exterminated by dusting with DDT between flushes.

Diseases

As only the plaster moulds—brown and white—are introduced in the compost, and all the other common diseases
with the casing soil (which has not had time to become re-
contaminated when used for filling in), the use of the almost
sterile peat and chalk mixture will ensure greater freedom
from disease. Brown plaster mould will be entirely eliminated
at a temperature of 126° F (52° C) so that correctly prepared
compost should be free of this disease. Again, it is usually an
excessively alkaline compost that will encourage white plaster
mould and this disease, too, will rarely become troublesome
in a well-prepared compost.

To prevent disease in the mushroom house, the ordinary
rules of sanitation should be observed. Excessively high
humidity should be guarded against, and this means that high
temperatures and lack of ventilation must not be permitted.

Pests and diseases

Diseases rarely become troublesome in a well-ventilated mushroom house. Sterilisation of the house after each crop must also be carried out as routine. In fact, where growing mushrooms nothing should be left to chance, for pest and disease can quickly wipe out what would appear to be a most successful crop.

Where disease does make its appearance on the beds it must be diagnosed as quickly as possible, so that the appropriate treatment may be undertaken. Diseased mushrooms should be removed without delay and burnt, for the spores may quite easily be carried to other beds in the same house, an inrush of air caused by an open ventilator being capable of spreading the spores about the house.

BACTERIAL PIT. The unattractive pitting of the caps of the mushrooms may be due to mites, for they are frequently to be found clustered in the pits. It may, however, be caused by bacteria introduced with the casing, which should be sterilised. Excessive humidity will encourage the trouble and, if observed, additional ventilation must be provided. The brown blotches or pits are coated with an unpleasant slimy substance which makes the mushrooms quite unsaleable.

BROWN PLASTER MOULD. This is *Papulaspora byssina*, which first appears as a white mould, later turning a bright brown colour. Like white plaster, it is a disease of the compost, wet and 'green' or under-composted manure being the main cause. Later it will work its way through to the casing soil, and though not so troublesome as white plaster mould, it must not be neglected.

Styer reports that the mould is killed when the compost reaches a temperature of 126° F (52° C). However, it is possible that the trouble is introduced after the beds have been lying dormant in woodwork or on the walls of the house. As with all diseases, prevention is better than cure, and no stone must be left unturned in cleaning the house and sterilising before each new crop is introduced. However, should brown plaster mould appear after the beds have been cased it will be necessary to remove not only the casing soil but also that part of the compost which is affected. The disease may be prevented from spreading by treating the infected area with a 2 per cent solution of formalin, and by replacing the soil and manure that have been removed by clean sterilised soil. Care should be taken in removing this mould, for under the microscope it appears as a minute bulb which is capable of throwing off millions of reproductive spores. All diseased mushrooms and infected areas should be burnt.

BROWN SPOT. *Verticillium malthousei* is also known as Dry Bubble Disease, and is becoming more troublesome than in previous years. The disease is similar in appearance to mycogone and is carried to the beds by spores in the casing soil. Mushroom flies appear to be the greatest source of infestation. The small mushrooms when attacked take on the form of the more common bubbles disease, except that no unpleasant liquid matter appears. The more developed mushroom shows this disease by brown spotting, cracking and peeling, and even swelling of the stalk.

To control the trouble all mushrooms attacked should be removed and burnt, and the humidity of the house should be reduced. This means keeping the beds as dry as possible without holding up production, and increasing ventilation. The disease may be prevented by dusting with Zibimate as for *Mycogone perniciosa*.

BUBBLES DISEASE. This is the dreaded *Mycogone perniciosa*, the most offensive and unfortunately the most prevalent of all fungus diseases, and may be present in any casing soil whatsoever. It is most disheartening to see an excellent

194

growth of mycelium in the compost and casing soil, only to find that, on appearance, the pin-head mushrooms take on the most grotesque shapes. As they become larger, the shapes begin to exude a brown, evil-smelling liquid. All affected mushrooms must be carefully removed and burnt at once, care being taken to wash the hands in disinfectant immediately afterwards.

That this disease is introduced with the casing soil is definite, but I have found that soil from a certain field and used immediately for casing has caused no signs of the disease to appear on the mushrooms, whereas the same soil which was left standing outside for two months before being used for casing another bed was highly contaminated and produced these ill-shaped mushrooms throughout the life of the bed. This seems to show that the disease is carried by either birds or insects or even by the wind. Areas of soil which never show signs of introducing the trouble may be used without fear of ruining the beds, but even so, sterilisation would eliminate any trouble that might be present. We know that mycogone is unable to withstand a period of one hour at a temperature of 122° F (50° C). Where sterilisation cannot be carried out, make certain that the casing soil is dug from well below the surface of the ground. For those who have not the necessary equipment for soil sterilisation by baking or by the steam-pressure method, the soil may be saturated with a 2 per cent solution of formalin and exposed to the elements for at least five weeks before being used on the beds. The soil should be turned each week to allow all fumes to escape.

Too humid an atmosphere will encourage the disease, so also will too frequent applications of water on the beds. Where attacks are noticed, water only when absolutely necessary, reduce the temperature of the house to 52° F (11° C) and give ample quantities of fresh air. It cannot be overstressed that too much humidity in a house is more often than not the cause of all the troubles associated with the mushrooms, and here it may be repeated that with detailed attention to the art of mushroom growing, from the moment the manure arrives until the beds are removed, there is no reason why any pest or disease should make itself a nuisance and the crop be anything other than profitable. Beds which have become badly affected should have their casing soil entirely removed and should be re-cased, though the trouble may be kept within bounds by carefully removing each infected mushroom as it appears and filling in the cavity with clean, sterilised soil containing a little lime.

Mr. H. M. Reed, the Hampshire grower, has reported that having had a first flush of mushrooms badly attacked by this disease in unsterilised casing soil, he removed every piece of growth. He then moved a flame gun over the remaining casing soil, and found that his next flush was almost completely free of mycogone.

In America it has been discovered that the dreaded mycogone disease may be controlled by first drying out the casing soil and then lowering the house temperature to around 50° F (10° C). Afterwards the beds are saturated (not so that the water will soak into the compost) with a strong Bordeaux Mixture. This is made by dissolving 1 lb. copper sulphate and 1 lb. quicklime in 50 gal. of water, a wooden tub being used owing to the corrosive action of the solution on metal. Control of Verticillium Disease, which takes a similar form to mycogone, is also said to be effective if treated with Bordeaux Mixture. The trouble may be prevented to a large degree by dusting the beds with Zibimate every ten days after casing. It should be used at a rate of 3 oz. per 1,000 sq. ft. of bed space.

COBWEB DISEASE. *Dactylium dendroides* is a disease that has not so far been nearly as troublesome as those already described, but I have known attacks on a small scale, and if not treated at once, the cobweb-like mycelium, which takes on a delicate pink shade, would rapidly make its way throughout the bed and so prevent the appearance of a full crop of mushrooms. Mushrooms which have been surrounded by cobweb disease turn brown and decay.

Again, the casing soil seems to be the source of trouble, which is carried either by insects or even by the air. To control the disease, reduce watering to a minimum and remove the casing soil wherever the trouble is located. Mr. F. C. Atkins, O.B.E., has said that bleaching powder and lime worked into the casing soil where the disease has been removed will do much to control the trouble.

Excessive moisture in the casing and high humidity of the house will encourage the disease to spread.

DAMPING OFF. This trouble is caused by the spores of *Fusarium oxysporum*, which may be introduced either with the casing, or with water supplies which may not be completely clean. The casing soil is the most frequent cause of the trouble and sterilisation will eliminate the risk, for the spores are destroyed by exposure for half an hour at a temperature of 150° F (66° C) or slightly higher.

If the spores are present in the soil they produce very fine mycelium threads. These give off a waste substance which competes with the mycelium of the pure culture mushroom spawn, rendering it incapable of producing a fully developed mushroom. It may be observed that the beds are full of spawn, but the pin-head mushrooms refuse to develop and gradually die away. This is caused by fusarium and is difficult to eradicate.

Dusting with hydrated lime will do much to prevent the disease making headway, but soil sterilisation is the only certain method of ensuring a healthy crop of mushrooms. If the infected areas are treated with 10 parts ammonium carbonate and 1 part copper sulphate, an ounce of which is dissolved in 1 gal. of water, this will do much to prevent the disease from spreading. Panning of the casing should also be prevented.

LA FRANCE DISEASE. This is now the most recent and most destructive of all mushroom diseases. It appeared first on the mushroom beds of the La France brothers in the United States in 1948, hence its name, and in Britain it was first noticed in 1955. It is also known as mushroom virus.

Where present, the mushrooms grow singly rather than in the usual clumps with long, curving stems and have small, light caps. In appearance the mushrooms are similar to those affected with mummy disease, though after a few days they emit the same slimy substance, but not the foul smell, as appears when mycogone is present. About a fortnight after its appearance the spawn in the beds appears to die back. The new Bitorquis spawn (see page 24) has proved immune to the disease and should be used where growing conditions are suitable. Otherwise provide conditions of utmost cleanliness.

MUMMY DISEASE. For long this has been a source of worry to American growers but only since 1950 has it become known to British growers. The first indications of it are when the pin-head mushrooms die back, and those which become affected, and have reached a more mature stage, have strangely thick bases and small, lop-sided caps which are leathery, whilst the gills are hard.

The trouble is thought to be a virus disease introduced into the casing soil, especially when the soil is either not sterilised or has been stacked for an undue length of time after being dug.

As yet it cannot be cured, only prevented from appearing or its progress halted when present. This is done by drying out the casing soil following a flush, and then removing the soil completely in the area where the disease has been noticed. The exposed compost should then be given a light spraying with a weak solution of formalin before fresh soil is replaced.

OLIVE-GREEN MOULD. *Chaetomium olivaceum* is only occasionally to be met with in mushroom beds, but surprisingly it is sometimes troublesome where the compost has been pasteurised at a temperature of more than 148° F (64° C). It is a mould of an olive-green colour, originating in the compost, and is sometimes present where the compost is wet and black and of an alkaline reaction, when it will grow at the expense of the spawn. There is no known cure, though additional ventilation will help to check it. The appearance of red pepper mites, which feed on the mould, is an indication that the disease is present in the compost.

TRUFFLE. *Diehliomyces microsporus* was first recorded in the United States of America in 1930, and in the British Isles in 1936. In the casing it forms dense, yellow, mycelium-like growth which turns to fruiting bodies, in appearance like yellow pin-head mushrooms, which turn brown in colour. The parasitic fungus feeds on the spawn and will soon reduce the compost to a sticky mass with a most unpleasant smell.

Truffle usually appears during the latter part of the life of a bed, when conditions become more acid and mycelium growth is weaker. For this reason it is important to enjoy heavy first flushes so that the beds do not occupy the house longer than necessary. In the United States Beach discovered that a temperature of 120° F (49° C) for 24 hours failed to kill the spores, and it is known that they have survived a compost heat temperature of as high as 140° F (60° C). It is, therefore, a most difficult disease to eradicate, though it is known that a *p*H value of the compost of over 7·5 prevents the appearance of the trouble. The continued fall in the pH value of a spawned bed, which causes the bed to become too acid for mushroom spawn growth, favours the truffle disease and brings cropping to an end. If any method could be found preventing this decline in pH value, a mushroom bed should continue to crop for ever and, at the same time, be immune from several all too common diseases. Here again, the correct composting of the manure should go a long way towards checking the appearance of the disease; a tightly packed soggy compost, as is often bedded down when gypsum has been omitted, tends to encourage the trouble. A considerable degree of control may be given by adding copper sulphate to the compost at the first turn, either in the liquid or granulated form, as when controlling vert-de-gris.

VERT-DE-GRIS. This is also known as Mat Disease and is caused by *Myceliophthora* spores, introduced with unsterilised soil. They cause a mat or layer to form between the compost and the casing soil. The thick, mycelium-like threads of the disease soon turn greenish-yellow in colour, growth becoming so dense that it prevents the spawn in the beds from penetrating to the casing.

At first it proved difficult to eradicate, for the spores are able to survive pasteurisation, and the high temperatures obtained when composting. The addition of 2 lb. of ground copper sulphate per ton of manure will, however, give protection against its appearance. I have always found this a most troublesome disease and not to be taken lightly, but the introduction of the copper sulphate has greatly improved cropping, whilst it will also prevent an outbreak of truffle and damping off disease.

WHITE PLASTER MOULD. *Scopulariopsis fimicola* is most active in a compost having a pH value of more than 7·0. In a too alkaline compost, such as often occurs when a black, sticky compost is bedded down, the mould tends to overcome the mushroom mycelium growth; but under very acid conditions, when the spawn itself would find difficulty in running, this disease is also unable to survive.

In 1937 Dr. Williams, of the Cheshunt Experimental Station, found that the disease could be controlled by removing the white mould from the casing soil and filling in the cavity with peat which has been saturated in a solution of 1 part acetic acid in 7 parts water. Over the top, fresh casing soil is placed and firmed down to the level of the surrounding soil.

Again, correct house humidity will play a big part in controlling the disease, and the use of gypsum in the compost will help to neutralise a too alkaline condition.

Checks should be made on the beds at frequent intervals from the time they have been cased, in order to apply the acetic acid treatment as soon as any signs of mould are seen.

Professor Pointing has discovered that watering the affected areas with a weak solution of superphosphate has given some control, whilst it is also noticed that the addition of several pounds of superphosphate to the manure during turning has tended to prevent any disastrous attacks of white plaster mould. It would, therefore, appear that if not given in excess, the addition of superphosphate has a definite importance quite apart from increased yield.

XYLARIA. *X. vaporaria* appears in both compost and soil as long black fleshy growths which may grow into pinkish branches as the crop appears. It is said that the disease is introduced with unsterilised casing soil, though I feel that it is introduced from the compost. Though only occasionally noticed, it will cause untold harm should it obtain a hold, and the disease should be removed as soon as observed by cutting out the growths with a knife and treating the cavity with lime before filling in with fresh sterilised soil.

15—Mushroom recipes

The value of mushrooms in the kitchen—recipes

The mushroom is a highly concentrated food, important for its protein, vitamin and folic acid content, unsurpassed for flavour in addition to being a completely satisfying meal. Those who cultivate their own mushrooms will take the crop in the condition of maturity as and when required. If mushrooms are required for pickling then they should be removed when they are in the button stage, before they reach cup-size, when they should be somewhere between the size of a five-pence piece and a ten-pence piece. The housewife who wishes to serve mushrooms as an omelet will generally use a mushroom with the gills just beginning to show underneath. In this state the mushroom is immensely succulent, but to my mind does not contain the tremendous aroma of a fully opened brown mushroom. Grilled on toast with cheese sauce poured over it will keep one going in the severest weather, especially if taken with a bottle of Guinness!

There is yet another great advantage of having your own mushrooms available at home: there will be mushrooms for all occasions, always fresh and succulent, with no waste whatsoever. It is the fact that they are completely devoid of waste that makes mushrooms, even at 60p a half pound, in winter an economical food.

To prepare mushrooms, the very end of the stalk may need

removal whilst the stalk may need a light scraping. It is then usual to remove the stalk altogether. Place stalk and cap in a bowl of cold water to remove any pieces of soil which may be attached, removing the mushrooms from the water as soon as possible. Drain on a cloth, and lightly peel the caps if they are of the brown variety. White mushrooms do not need peeling. Any peeling should be done immediately before they are to be used, for they quickly become dehydrated. The peelings and any pieces of stalk removed may be used for sauces. It should not be necessary to discard any part.

The attractive whiteness of mushrooms may be retained in their cooking by the addition of a few drops of lemon juice to the water in which they are cleaned.

Recipes
Preserving mushrooms. Not that there will be any left for this purpose if you cultivate only one or two boxes, but the grower who might be lucky in obtaining heavy flushes on outdoor beds or in pasture will find dried mushrooms most useful for winter and spring dishes or for flavouring.

The mushrooms are best skinned, removing the thin layer covering the cap, holding the stalk with the other hand. Some prefer to discard the stalk and dry only the caps, which are spread out on trays and placed in an airing cupboard or a slightly warmed oven until they appear quite dry and shrivelled. When cool, they may be stored in tins or, if a skewer is pushed through the cap of each, they may be threaded with string and hung up in a dry, cool place until they are required for use. Dried mushrooms retain almost their full flavour for sauces, stews, etc. They must be soaked before using.

Pickled mushrooms. There is no more tasty addition to the table than fresh button mushrooms pickled in best malt

vinegar. With cold meats they provide a most appetising
flavour and are like eating succulent nuts. In fact, it is little
use pickling only one jar, for the first mushroom eaten is the
signal for 'no stopping' until the jar is emptied. Use only
small pots or jars, for one can rarely pickle more than two or
three on account of the cost if bought in the shops, or the fact
that mushrooms are always wanted for the main dish on the
table. Never wash mushrooms; to do so would be like washing the bloom off grapes or peaches; just place them in a
saucepan and cover them with a little salt. Place over a very
low flame or, better still, leave them on the hob in front of a
fire until the moisture begins to leave them, then cover with
malt vinegar, and allow the whole to simmer for five minutes.
They are then ready for placing in small pots and should be
covered and made airtight when cold. Store in a cool place
until ready. Keep a jar until Christmas to have with cold
turkey; the flavour of the turkey and pungent aroma of the
pickled mushrooms makes for a superb meal.

Mushroom omelet. There are ways of cooking the mushroom
other than the everlasting grilling or cooking in milk. An
omelet takes five minutes and for one person this is the procedure: Chop up three small mushrooms, or even one large
one, and place them in a pan. Add to the mushrooms 1 oz. of
margarine (or butter if preferred) and a little salt and pepper.
Simmer this mixture gently. Make up and fry the omelet
mixture and when ready add the simmered mushrooms,
fold over and cook for another few seconds, then serve
piping hot. The aroma from the mushrooms can be smelled
several doors away. A good big brown mushroom is, to my
mind, far superior to the large buttons so often used for
this purpose.

Stuffed mushrooms. As a change from the large grilled mushrooms, try stuffing two or three large cup mushrooms, with

their gills showing an attractive deep pink colour. Remove the stems and mince these with a little parsley and, if you like the flavour, add a small onion. Add salt and pepper and cook in 1 oz. of margarine. Beat up an egg and to this add a pinch of breadcrumbs, stirring this into the simmering mushroom stalks. As soon as the whole is thickened, place in the mushroom caps and bake for four to five minutes, making your toast at the same time so that the whole may be served piping hot.

Mushrooms and eggs. As an alternative to meat dishes or even sausages, which are now expensive, there are several ways of serving mushrooms and eggs together. Hens in the yard, mushrooms in the cellar, tomatoes in the greenhouse, and apples in store will supply the household with nourishing meals the whole year round. During summer, when plentiful, tomatoes can accompany many mushroom dishes, especially during July and August when tomatoes are most abundant and mushrooms too, are at their cheapest. In September come field mushrooms and there is often a 'glut' after a hot, dry summer. At this time, mushrooms and eggs make an inexpensive and nourishing meal. Even at 6p for a large egg, and a few mushrooms costing about 10p, together with a little margarine, these foods are relatively cheap.

For poached egg and mushrooms in one, a good, hefty, brown mushroom is the most tasty. It should be peeled, cut into shreds and placed in a saucepan with ½ oz. of margarine or dripping and left to simmer. Put on the lid to retain the flavour and keep it moist. Have your buttered toast ready and a poached egg waiting. Place the mushrooms on the toast and on top place the egg. A little chopped parsley, and salt and pepper, will provide a meal 'fit for the gods'.

Stuffed potatoes. Here is another cheap meal when you have field mushrooms available, or you grow your own. This is yet another dish, highly satisfying and most delicious, which will save the meat until the weekend. It is economical and a way of using up any large flat mushrooms which may have been left on the beds over the weekend.

Take several good-sized potatoes, peel them and cut off the tops. Hollow out the insides and fill them with mushrooms that have been chopped and allowed to simmer as previously described. When the mushrooms are cooked, place them in the potatoes, standing them upright in an oven dish. Put a little margarine or fat over them, and remove to a hot oven and allow them to remain there until cooked through and browned. Serve with juice poured over them and with cooked tomatoes if they are on hand, or a rasher of bacon. A grand meal for a cold autumn day and wonderful for school children.

Mushroom soup. This is one of the most delicious of all soups and can be served, even when mushrooms are to be used for another course as a savoury, for it must be remembered that few people grow their own mushrooms and so rarely have the opportunity of tiring of their flavour. Mushroom soups must have white-capped and pink-gilled mushrooms, for the big dark brown ones will spoil the appearance of the soup. A ¼ lb. of mushrooms should be used for soup for four people and they should be sliced, seasoned and allowed to simmer with 1 oz. of margarine added for about five minutes. A good pint of stock should then be added to the simmering mushrooms and the whole allowed to simmer for nearly an hour. The liquid must then be strained and returned to the stock pot, and an ounce of flour mixed with a little milk is then added, together with a half-cupful of chopped parsley. Simmer again, then, if it can be spared, ½ pt. of cream taken from the top of the milk should be stirred in, a little more salt and pepper added and the whole left simmering until ready for use. This is a most nourishing soup for every occasion.

Mushroom recipes

Mushroom sauce will help to add interest to the winter meals when home-grown mushrooms are in short supply. Here, the mushrooms are better if they are brown and over-matured. They should be peeled, cut up into small pieces and placed in a casserole dish in layers with salt sprinkled between. Then simmer for approximately eight hours over the lowest possible flame or on a warm hot-plate. A few cloves and a little ginger may be added as required, whilst the simmering is in progress. The mushrooms should then be pressed tightly to extract the maximum amount of liquid, which should then be strained off, boiled for 20 minutes and bottled as soon as cool. Take care when adding spices, use very few, for the mushroom flavour is potent on its own.

Mushrooms with salad. Mushrooms are most tasty when eaten raw. They are just like nuts, and I often pop a 'button' in my mouth whilst working in the mushroom houses. They make a tasty salad in hot weather if they are cut into shreds and mixed with a dressing of olive oil and vinegar to bring out the flavour. A little garlic or a chopped shallot, a tomato and some chopped parsley and plenty of crisp, chopped lettuce will make a delicious summer salad.

Mushroom roll. Place ½ lb. of minced bacon in the frying pan, begin to fry and add a small chopped onion and several chopped matured mushrooms. Mix in some herbs and fry for three or four minutes. A suet crust should previously have been made and this is rolled out so that it may be covered with a thin layer of the fry mixture. Then roll the pastry and tie in a cloth to be steamed for 2½ hours. Serve in thick slices with grilled tomatoes and tomato sauce.

Mushroom and spinach roulade. This is one of Miss Rosemary Hume's excellent recipes. Stewed spinach is placed in a saucepan containing a little butter and is cooked for a few minutes. Mix in the yolks of four eggs and a little grated cheese. Whip the whites of the eggs and fold into the spinach, using, of course, a metal spoon. Spread on to a tin and bake in a moderately hot oven for ten minutes. As it is cooking, $\frac{1}{4}$ lb. of mushrooms are prepared by boiling in a mixture of $\frac{1}{2}$ oz. of butter, a large teaspoonful of flour, and milk and seasoning. The mushroom filling is spread out on the soufflé which is rolled up and served piping hot without delay.

Mushroom and fish pie. Boil several small onions and chop them. Mix with 1 oz. of butter and a heaped teaspoonful of flour, and bake for ten minutes in a moderate oven. Peel $\frac{1}{4}$ lb. of mushrooms and rub through a coarse sieve. Heat another 1 oz. of butter to which is added the mushroom purée and a few drops of lemon juice. Cook for ten minutes, then add the onion mixture. Line a buttered casserole dish with several small fish fillets and cover with half the mushroom mixture, then add more fillets and the remainder of the mixture, finally covering with mashed potato. Bake for about 20 minutes in a moderate oven. The result will be a most delicious and satisfying meal.

Mushroom savoury. A most tasty savoury may be made by cutting a half-slice of toast into three strips, over which are placed small rashers of fried bacon. These are covered with tiny open mushrooms which have been fried with the bacon. Dozens of these little mushrooms will be available when the crop comes towards its end and they are most suitable used for savouries.

Mushroom surprise. Chop a small onion and about 2 oz. of mushrooms and lightly fry. Chop up some parsley and mix with breadcrumbs, add the onion and mushroom mixture and bind with an egg. Then on to four rashers of bacon, place some of the mixture. Fold and hold in position with a skewer. Grill for about five minutes with a few more mushrooms and serve on fried bread or toast.

Mushroom recipes

Baked mushrooms. Select several large cup-sized mushrooms and remove the stalks. Place them, gills uppermost, in a glass fireproof dish, cover with cream, a squeeze of lemon juice and season with salt and pepper, then transfer to a hot oven, after placing over them a lid or cover. Bake for 30 minutes and serve immediately.

Curry mushrooms. First fry two sliced onions in butter and add ½ lb. peeled and sliced tomatoes and simmer until reduced to a pulp. Then add 2 teaspoonfuls of curry powder and 1 of salt; simmer for another 5 minutes. Add ½ pt. of stock bring to the boil and simmer for another 20 minutes. Then add ½ lb. mushrooms, mix thoroughly and simmer for a further 20 minutes. Serve at once.

Mushrooms à l'Arlesienne. A delicious French recipe. To 1 lb. of mushrooms add ½ lb. tomatoes, peeled and quartered. Place in a fireproof dish, add a teaspoonful of finely chopped onion and one of parsley, the juice of a lemon and season with salt and pepper. Add 1 teaspoonful of olive oil and bake in a hot oven for 30 minutes. Serve as soon as ready.

Mushrooms à la Bordelaise. Take 1 lb. of mature mushrooms and remove the stalks, then place the caps in a frying pan containing 4 oz. of hot olive oil. Add 1 oz. of chopped onion and fry for about 15 minutes, turning over the mushrooms continually so that both sides are evenly done. Remove and serve at once, sprinkling them first with chopped parsley.

Paprika mushrooms. Chop two good sized onions and fry till brown, then add ¾ lb. small mushrooms, and barely cover with water. Season with salt and a tablespoon of paprika. Cover the saucepan and simmer gently till the mushrooms are tender, during which time the water will have evaporated. Stir in half a cupful of cream and serve immediately.

Mushroom vol-au-vent. First prepare the mushrooms by placing ½ lb. of buttons in six tablespoons of water, a sprink-

209

ling of salt and the juice of half a lemon. Bring to the boil and add 1 oz. butter. Boil for 5 minutes when the mushrooms will be ready to use. Place two or three in a case of puff pastry, add a dash of Mornay sauce, cover with a pastry lid and place in a hot oven for 10 minutes until thoroughly warmed through. Serve at once with peas and new potatoes.

Mushroom flan. Line a flan tin with puff pastry and cover it with about 2 lb. of mushrooms (small 'flats' are best) which have been boiled. This is done by placing the mushrooms in a saucepan, after removing all but a $\frac{1}{2}$ in. of stalk. Pour in a small cupful of water, add a good pinch of salt and the juice of half a lemon. Cover the mushrooms with 1 oz. of butter or margarine and boil for about 5 minutes—mushrooms become tough if allowed to cook for too long. If available, sprinkle the mushrooms when in the flan with a few spoonfuls of stock and decorate in squares with thin strips of puff pastry. Brush them with beaten egg yolk and place the flan in a brisk oven until the pastry has turned light brown. Serve hot from the oven with a rasher of bacon.

Mushroom pancakes. Make unsweetened pancakes, adding a pinch of salt to the batter. When cooked, cover with chopped mushrooms prepared as described in recipe for mushroom flan. Whilst piping hot, fold the pancake and serve with lemon juice. The pancakes can be accompanied by sauté potatoes or brown bread and butter.

Glossary

Activator A preparation especially manufactured for converting straw into a suitable mushroom growing compost.

Casing Covering the spawned compost with suitable materials, into which the mycelium threads can fuse together to produce the fruiting body, i.e. the mushroom.

Compost The material used for mushroom production.

Flush The term used for the appearance of the mushrooms at intervals of about ten days.

Fumigation The eradication of pests and diseases from mushroom houses by means of gases released from chemical compounds.

Gas Layer Where ventilation is inadequate, heavy gases collect above the casing, having adverse effects on the growing crop.

Grain Spawn So called where the mycelium has been used to inoculate grains of wheat, barley or rye; it is mostly used where growing under the tray system.

Greasy Compost A condition which may be the result of a badly prepared compost, setting like lard in the beds (or boxes) and cutting off the necessary air supplies to the growing spawn. Such a compost will usually have a 'green' or black appearance.

Moist Spawn Spawn which has not been dried and is fully active so that it grows away rapidly when planted, and so

211

crops earlier. It should be used as soon as received and is for the more experienced grower.

Mycelium Spawn threads which spread out from the inserted spawn to permeate the compost, later fusing to form the mushroom.

Over-Composting A condition caused by too long a preparation of the compost, resulting in a reduced crop.

Pasteurisation See Peak Heating.

Peak Heating Also known as pasteurisation, and is used to bring the compost, immediately after it has been made into beds, to a temperature of between 130° and 140° F (54° and 60° C) to sweeten it and absorb any excess moisture, whilst also driving any pests to the surface to be killed by fumigation.

*p*H Test The means by which the acidity or alkalinity of a soil or compost is determined.

Site Contamination Similar to soil sickness in its cause and cure. Where mushrooms have been growing in a house or shed for any length of time, crops begin to diminish unless treatment is provided.

Smoke Generator A method used for mushroom house fumigation. The generator is self-contained, and all that is required is to light the wick and seal the house.

Soil Sickness A condition created by successive crops contaminating the soil of caves, rhubarb houses or greenhouses resulting in reduced crops. It can be cured by sterilisation.

Spawning The planting of mushroom spawn in the prepared compost.

Synthetic Composts Composts made from organic or inorganic compounds as alternatives to horse or other animal manures.

Through Spawning The method by which grain spawn is

212

used, being spread over the surface of the compost, which is then made loose with a fork so that the spawn grains reach down into the compost.

Tiers Method of growing mushrooms in tier beds raised above the floor and made of angle iron or wood.

Trashing Removing pieces of decayed root and stem following the gathering of a flush of mushrooms.

Trays Wooden containers suitable for growing mushrooms, which are usually of a size to make for easy handling.

Under-Composting When compost has not been sufficiently prepared.

Index

Activator, its use, 38, 41, 44, 72, 94, 112, 115, 211
Air extraction, 58
Allen, P. G., 100
Atkins, F. C., 197

Bacterial activity, 40, 41, 68, 69, 74, 81, 83, 87, 111
Beds, mushroom
  filling in, 51, 149, 170
  making, 49, 98
  outdoors, 165
  spawning, 122, 123, 125, 168, 212
  temperature of, 49
  their casing, 50, 64, 127, 128, 169
  their cropping, 46, 138, 147, 149
  their inspection, 127
  their watering, 51, 138, 142, 147
  trashing, 149, 157, 170, 213
  when to make up, 46, 95
  yields of, 100, 105, 111, 131, 137
Bewley, Dr., 131, 133
Boxes (trays), for mushrooms, 25, 54, 56, 213
  care of, 143, 145
  construction of, 31, 56
  filling, 45, 100, 104
  obtaining, 28, 56
  pasteurisation of, 104, 125
  preserving, 31
  size of, 56
  spawning, 125
  sterilization of, 51, 178

Carbon dioxide, 36, 58, 102, 127, 144
Casing, 50, 128, 131, 137, 211
  correct depth of, 50, 137, 138, 143
  correct time for, 49, 129
  materials for, 50, 129, 131, 135
  reasons for, 128
  ridge beds, 168
  texture of, 50, 133
Cellar, its use, 31, 45
Chalk, for casing, 64, 129, 135
Compost
  appearance of, 45, 68, 95
  bedding down, 48, 95
  by artificial methods, 40, 42, 45, 68, 105, 114, 212
  greasy, 211
  its preparation, 37, 40, 43, 46, 79, 88, 96, 211

  its removal, 62, 177
  peak heating of, 54, 102, 212
  pH testing of, 89, 90, 92, 103, 199
  site, 63
  temperature of, 41, 43, 48
Materials for
  ammonium sulphate, 114
  calcium cyanide, 117
  dried blood, 72, 114
  potassium chloride, 117
  preparations for synthetic, 111
  sulphate of potash, 82
  superphosphate, 82
  urea, 68, 114, 116
Concrete, for composting, 62
  for floors, 55, 62

Diseases:
  Bacterial pit, 193
  Brown plaster mould, 74, 183, 193
  Brown spot, 194
  Cobweb, 184, 196
  Damping off, 197
  La France, 198
  Mummy, 198
  Mushroom virus, 24, 198
  Mycogone perniciosa ('Bubbles'), 50, 131, 140, 183, 194
  Olive-green mould, 68, 199
  Truffle, 183, 199
  Vert-de-gris, 183, 200
  White plaster mould, 74, 200
  Xylaria, 201

Falck, 67
Falconer, 88
Fibre glass, 34, 53, 55
Flegg, P. B., 128
Frame, its construction, 31
  its use, 31, 170
Frank, Dr. Benjamin, 21
Fungicides:
  Bordeaux Mixture, 196
  Copper naphthnate, 31
  copper sulphate, 200
  Cuprinol, 56
  ECA-55, 178
  Formalin, 51, 61, 140, 176, 188, 194, 195
  Sterilite, 141
  SterIzal, 51, 184
  Zibimate, 184, 194, 196

214

Index

215